P9-ELW-498

THE CANINE CLAN

Also by John C. McLoughlin

THE ANIMALS AMONG US

ARCHOSAURIA

SYNAPSIDA

THE TREE OF ANIMAL LIFE

THE CANINE CLAN

A New Look at Man's Best Friend

JOHN C. McLOUGHLIN

THE VIKING PRESS
NEW YORK

Copyright © 1983 by John C. McLoughlin
All rights reserved
First published in 1983 by The Viking Press
625 Madison Avenue, New York, N.Y. 10022
Published simultaneously in Canada by
Penguin Books Canada Limited

Grateful acknowledgment is made to Houghton Mifflin Company and Konrad Lorenz for permission to reprint a selection from *Man Meets Dog* by Konrad Lorenz. Copyright © 1953 by Konrad Lorenz.

Library of Congress Cataloging in Publication Data
McLoughlin, John C.
The canine clan.
Bibliography: p.
Includes index.
1. Canidae. 2. Dogs. I. Title.
QL737.C22M39 1982 599.74'442 81-65280
ISBN 0-670-20264-9 AACR2

Printed in the United States of America
Set in Linotype Granjon

CONTENTS

PREFACE vii

ACKNOWLEDGMENTS xiv

THE MEANING OF MAMMALHOOD 3

THE RISE OF THE CARNIVORES 12

THE WORLD OF MAMMALIAN CARNIVORES 19

THE RISE OF THE CANIDAE 27

REYNARD THE TRICKSTER AND OTHER FOXY TYPES 45

THE WILD HUNTING DOGS 58

GENUS *CANIS* 69

DOMESTICATION 83

EARLY PHYLOGENY OF DOMESTIC BREEDS 94

MASTIFFS 105

MIDGETS AND DWARVES 116

CANIDS IN THE WORLD OF MAN 130

APPENDIX: LIVING CANID GENERA AND SPECIES 142

GLOSSARY 145

BIBLIOGRAPHY 151

INDEX 152

To my parents,
Comerford Whitehouse McLoughlin and
Elizabeth Merrill McLoughlin,
this book is gratefully dedicated

PREFACE

One day, during a hard winter, a deer crossed our snowed-up garden fence and was torn to pieces by my three dogs. As I stood horror-stricken by the mutilated corpse I became conscious of the unconditional faith which I placed in the social inhibition of these blood-thirsty beasts, for my children were at that time smaller and more defenceless than the deer whose gory remains lay before me in the snow. I was myself astonished at the absolute fearlessness with which I daily entrusted the fragile limbs of my children to the wolflike jaws.

—Konrad Lorenz, *Man Meets Dog*

Lying beside me is a predator weighing about 35 kilograms, baring in his sleep a set of recurved teeth designed specifically to rend the flesh and crack the bones of large animals. Along comes my daughter, Ariana, four years of age and weighing about 20 kilograms, looking for trouble as must all healthy children of her age. Aha! Here sleeps the big hairy beast, almost twice her weight and countless times her equal in strength and swiftness—but, in sleep, defenseless. Ariana hurls herself onto the sleeping form, her weight driving a grunt from the animal's lungs—and he awakens, nosing her face affectionately before rolling clumsily onto his back, paws in the air, eager at once for such abuse as the child can dish out.

An ordinary scene, familiar to any owner of a large dog; and yet, as Dr. Lorenz remarks, it is indeed strange that such a superb and efficient predator is so willing to endure insult and perhaps even injury in the name of play with weaker and dissimilar beings. An extraterrestrial intelligence, unfamiliar with our ways, might wonder long and hard that the human being, defenseless without the aid of artificial weaponry, infantile even in adulthood, has such an ally as the domestic dog, descendant of wolves, physically designed for carnage.

Domestication, the symbiosis between human beings and other organisms to produce new and man-made species, is a brand-new phenomenon as evolutionary processes go. Almost all domesticated plants and animals have originated within the past 12,000 or so years, and most more recently than that. The domestic dog, *Canis familiaris*, is by far the oldest domesticate, enjoying a symbiosis with human beings that stretches back perhaps 50,000 years; even this vast interval, however, is but a thin skin at the top of the evolution-

ary history of his family, a history that uniquely predisposed him for the position in the first place. It is, in fact, hard to say which species—human or canine—first initiated the process of domestication.

Of course, most breeds of domestic dogs have their origin in some sort of specialized work. Hunting dogs, dogs of war and the chase, herders, and guards have shared our history in a bewildering array of forms and temperaments selected by human beings to further their own ends. Most recently in their long history, domestic dogs have taken on the specialized function—independent of work—of being friends and companions to their human symbiotes; this last, perhaps, is the most astonishing relationship between two such disparate forms.

Further examination of the story, however, reveals this complex alliance to be a natural outgrowth of a set of very basic similarities between members of the human family, the Hominidae, and that of the dogs, the Canidae. Illustrating these similarities is the fact that any wild canid intelligently raised by people from infancy displays affection toward his human custodians. This is especially true of those canids whose natural bent is toward sociability—such as wolves, whose wild state is one of community within familial groups of their own kind. These social canids, commonly grouped together as "wild dogs," themselves represent but one facet of the family Canidae; some thirty-six species of canids within twelve genera (depending on which of the many current classifications one favors) share our world today. Considered together with the many extinct canid forms, these constitute a remarkably homogeneous family—even a little child can recognize its boundaries clearly—and yet is represented in its natural state by such variety in form and function that nondomesticated canids occupy every climate and all of the world's continents except Australia and Antarctica. All are intelligent, second among land mammals only to the higher primates like ourselves, and all are therefore extremely adaptable. To this adaptability the Canidae owe their immense range and success, and it is specifically on this canid canniness and its history that this book hinges.

We live on a planet dominated by our species, *Homo sapiens*. For better or for worse, human beings have altered, and at an accelerating rate continue to alter, our world. Less and less space remains for undomesticated mammals bigger than, say, rats, and thus fewer and fewer people are able to grasp a sense of the earth as it once was, an arena within which many parallel forms of intelligence evolved and might have continued to evolve. Human beings ended all that; as the first tool users, they began to eliminate potentially competing higher intelligences in a process that continues to this day with the approaching disappearance of the manlike primates and all intelligent wild predators including even the whales of the ocean. Once these bright beings are gone, we will be pretty much alone here. Whose mind will we share in that lonely time, only a few decades hence?

Why, that of the dog, of course. Alone among comparable intelligences, his is likely to share the world with us for some time to come. As a satellite of our kind, the dog is the only mammal besides the rat and mouse and domesticated cat to share the entire global range of humanity. Dogs even entered outer space before human beings did, and will likely follow them there in the future. Truly, the human and canid minds are shared; without such sharing there would be no symbiosis between them as complete as that we see today. It is no cynical exaggeration to say that dogs can be "man's best friend"; as an example, evidence mounts that the life of an elderly person may be prolonged by the presence of a dog. Physically healthy retirees from large corporations, long accustomed to functioning as part of their organizations, are at the time of their retirement confronted with a new sense of purposelessness that can reduce their life spans considerably. Such persons die of heart failure, stroke, and cancers that are mysteriously absent in many of their contemporaries of worse physical habits but more independently motivated life-styles. Increasingly we come to realize that the sense of uselessness is fatal to human beings.

Ah, but one is never useless to his dog. Barbarically abandoned by employers, by children, left adrift by the death of friends, the elder can still share his time with a dog. As a result, victims of the uselessness-related diseases are often markedly improved in health by taking on a dog, this being especially the case among heart patients. Here we see a renewal of the human need to interact and share, a resurgence accomplished through the intelligent awareness that is the hallmark of the canid brain. In this case the dog is indeed "man's best friend," and what a sordid commentary on the treatment by modern society of its elders is this substitution of canine for human affection!

This is, of course, but one of many examples of the dog's unique function as an intelligent mirror to our lives, a function central to the companionable aspect of the hominid-canid symbiosis. Regarded in this light, dogs become "people," too, in many ways more humane than human beings. Nowhere is this aspect of the canid potential more visible than in the choices by human beings of their canine companions. It is often remarked that some persons resemble their dogs, much as they tend to resemble their human friends in interests and temperament: birds of a feather flock together. Dog lovers tend to favor certain breeds over the years because they have proven best to mirror the owners' lives. As classic stereotypes of such relationships, I might cite the stout Bavarian with his dachshund, the long-haired dancer with her Afghan hound, and the portly matron with her Pekingese.

As another example, I prefer large, lanky mutts, probably because I am the human equivalent of such animals (being myself large and lanky and of questionable Nordic-Celtic background). I like the varieties of dog with erect, wolfish ears as opposed to floppy ones, and I like dogs with alert and curious ways rather than the more dependent canine varieties; this is likely so because it is my business and livelihood to be interested in the goings-on of the natural world. Thus my current mongrel, a real product of my New Mexico homeland. Foxy red-gold in color, Rufus stems from a line bred by a family of friends of mine, Hispanic trappers and goatherds from a small town near Santa Fe. This dog enjoys in his ancestry the admixture of genes from a domestically raised coyote bitch who was removed from her den as a pup. Experimentally bred to the German shepherd dogs of her captors three dog generations back, she lives on in Rufus in the form of a certain craftiness and stealth unusual in big dogs. His amber eyes and lightness of build may also reflect her part in his lineage, as may his generally unruly and lazy egg-sucking personality as a whole.

But Rufus sucks no eggs unless I give them to him, for he is a town dog.

Nor does he kill sheep, although I suspect he would if he could find them. Nonetheless, he does manage somehow to adorn our yard with the heads of goats and other spectacularly unattractive refuse of the town in total disregard of my efforts to improve his taste. Mere dogfood of the commercial variety is anathema to Rufus by way of food, and he will cheerfully skip a day or two of eating if this stuff is all that is offered—yet he gorges on cellophane and paper if these be ever so slightly tainted by the scent of some long-gone, putrescent sausage.

Such a dog can only be a companion. If he understood the word, the mere mention of "work" would probably bring on a sudden fit of canine ague. To be sure, he is minimally useful as a deterrent to unwanted visitors, both in his formidable appearance and in his delight at noisily cornering those (like religious proselytizers and salespeople) who have no honest business here. But this is not work to Rufus; it is play, as all life was meant to be.

No, Rufus is not here because he is useful in a material sense. He is here primarily because as a friend and as an animal he is an interesting adornment to the life of our family. An "ornamental carnivore," I like to call him, a luxury like the equally useless family cats. My love for such "useless" beings stems in large part from my appreciation of their sensory awareness, so different from our own, and their incredible *readability*. Every twitch of muscle, every movement of the antennalike ears, every curl of the lip in sensing the wind speaks clearly of the inner workings of Rufus's agile little brain, such that a simple walk with him becomes an expansion of my own consciousness as I share his responses to the world about us.

And I enjoy these big mutts for their involvement with children. At four, my daughter is herself still something of a primal being, whose inclinations toward hunting and gathering are as yet undiminished by peer pressure and the deadly television dementia. Walking with her and the dog, I see and hear far more than I could alone; together they form an eager symbiotic creature through whose collective senses I can catch a glimpse of our gorgeous past before the rise of bureaucracy and the conforming influences of the State. In short, the dog can function as a sort of instrument of understanding, an enlarger of the mind.

Which brings us back to the original domestication of canids. The process began with a growing alliance in the hunt, an alliance due to the canid possession of running speed and certain senses useful in long-distance, non-visual location of prey—advantages at that time unavailable to human hunters. Humans, on the other hand, possessed superb vision and the ability to attack giant prey; characteristically, they killed more than they ate. Thus as the econiches of human beings and the ancestral dogs converged, both species were benefited and the symbiosis broadened. It could not have begun, however, unless the biologic histories of man and wild dog had not in advance suited them to alliance.

Here we will attempt to trace the evolutionary history leading to this alliance, from a foundation in the misty past of 200,000,000 years ago to its present incarnation in the multifarious breeds of domesticated canids. Here, the dog will be considered not only as "man's best friend" but as a member of the family Canidae, the product of millions of years of natural selection. Within this broader framework, a novel classification of domestic breeds is erected—based not on function (as is traditionally done with "working," "toy," "sporting," "hound," and other groups) but on genetic origin within the human cultural context. Seen in this light, the long canid history offers a tale of beauty and grandeur seldom approached in examinations of domestic dogs alone. Because these latter are but recent and momentary expressions of the evolution of the Canidae, they make their entrance at the end of the book. Still, our dogs are windows on the disappearing wild; this book is best read in the company of a dog.

ACKNOWLEDGMENTS

In addition to the scholars of dogdom whose names appear in the text and bibliography of this book, my thanks go to Barbara Burn, whose seemingly endless patience has seen this and many another of my books to completion; to my wife, Carole Crews McLoughlin, who puts up with all the unlikely creatures—human, canid, and other—sharing our abode through the years; and to my daughter, Ariana Merrill McLoughlin, an inspiration in any enterprise.

THE CANINE CLAN

THE MEANING OF MAMMALHOOD

At first glance, the placid family dog may seem to betray little of his remarkable lineage. However, his presence in our houses and hearts takes on a new and far broader significance when viewed in the light of his noble ancestry, for first and foremost he and all his cousins among the Canidae are carnivorous mammals. Each of these appellations, "carnivore" and "mammal," represents a delightful story in itself, not only of our dogs but of our own minds and the path along which we came, so that we could write and read books like this. For amusement's sake, then, we will begin tracing the dog's family tree by ambling backward some hundreds of millions of years in time to an era in which the earth was populated by animals and plants of diverse sorts rarely seen outside museums and madhouses today.

Mammals are those animals belonging in the class Mammalia of "warm-blooded" vertebrates who suckle their young on milk from skin glands called mammae (Latin for "breasts"). Because we are endothermic—"heated-from-within" by physiological processes rather than by our surroundings—most of us mammals must conserve our internal heat by means of some sort of bodily insulation; thus we sport a variety of furry or fatty body coverings responsible for another common moniker for most terrestrial members of our class, the "furbearers."

The above definitions are useful when applied to living mammals, and they enable us to distinguish such forms as bats (flying mammals) from the birds with whom they share the air, or whales (swimming mammals) from the fishes with whom they share the seas. However, the mammalian story goes back more than 200,000,000 years, and from those remote times we are left only a few bones and teeth with which to piece the tale together. Such rem-

A mammalian sampler. *Left to right*: a bat, a man and dog, a blue whale, a wallaby. Their different forms and functions testify to the great success with which mammals have invaded all manner of econiches.

---

nants say little about either fur or mammary glands, and scientists working with them have been forced to set an arbitrary skeletal line of demarcation between "mammals" and "premammals" in the fossil record. It is often said, therefore, that mammals are "those animals whose jaws articulate with their skulls through a dentary-squamosal joint, rather than through an articular-quadrate joint as in 'reptiles' "!

While that mouthful of jargon may seem merely a pomposity on the part of the scientific establishment, it is actually a convenient way in which we may refer to the elegant process by which mammals distill energy from their food, a process distinguishing them sharply from all of their nonmammalian relatives. In fact, the jaw-joint position is ultimately responsible for the existence

of the unique mammalian intelligence with which dogs and human beings are so abundantly gifted.

The reptilelike animals from which dogs and people are descended have been dubbed *synapsids* by paleontologists. This name refers to the conformation of the heads of these long-gone beasts, in particular to an opening in the back of the skull around which play the muscles of the jaws. Synapsids originated around 300,000,000 years ago, when vertebrates were first invading the land in a big way. During this period of colonization, changing environmental conditions increasingly pressed the pioneers toward an ability to maintain themselves at a fairly constant operating temperature in order that they might get the jump on their less efficient contemporaries. The resultant competition produced some truly wonderful animals in a great synapsid adaptive radiation—an invasion by these new animals of a multitude of new forms and ways of life—that was the first to fill the heretofore vacant land econiches available to vertebrates. All this occurred between about 265,000,000 and 230,000,000 years ago.

Because most of them were quite unlike anything living today, synapsids and their ways are hard to envision across the vast gulf of time separating them from us, their descendants. Nonetheless, we are able to trace in their evolution a growing ability to use food energy more efficiently, with a consequently growing independence from direct solar heating of the primitive sort still exhibited by reptiles. This process is especially apparent in the changes incurred by synapsid jaw structure, which shows a gradual strengthening and simplification reflective of their growing ability to process food quickly.

By around 230,000,000 years ago, a wide variety of vegetarian, insectivorous, and meat-eating synapsids of an advanced group called therapsids, "beastlike ones," dominated the earth's continental life. However, the rise of another group, the dinosaurs, took place at the very height of synapsid diversity and eventually resulted in the latter's downfall. Like synapsids, dinosaurs owed their conquest of the terrestrial world to their growing energy efficiency; dinosaurs, however, arrived at this level of efficiency through another route, by which, descending from crocodilelike swamp dwellers, they early became agile, erect, birdlike bipeds (birds, indeed, may be regarded as small flying dinosaurs, much as bats are regarded as small flying mammals).

An advanced therapsid (*left*) and an early dinosaur. The superior speed and agility of dinosaurs permitted them to usurp the econiches of therapsids, driving the latter group into extinction. Therapsids left little nocturnal mammals as their descendants, however, and these meek insect-eaters emerged at the beginning of the Cenozoic to inherit the earth.

Synapsids, on the other hand, were for the most part rather clumsy animals by modern standards. Their legs splayed from their bodies in a manner reminiscent of those of lizards, so that they were constrained to live far closer to the ground than did the swift dinosaurs. Being much slower and less agile, synapsids could not compete successfully with dinosaurs, and the latter half of the Triassic period, around 185,000,000 years ago, saw their gradual replacement by the rising dinosaur dynasty. So efficient were the dinosaurs that they sat at the tops of most terrestrial food chains for some 140,000,000 years. During that colossal interval, the longest such ascendancy of any terrestrial vertebrate class including our own, dinosaurs successfully occupied most land econiches that are today tenanted by mammals.

While synapsids were replaced, however, they by no means left no descendants. The squeeze forced on their kind by dinosaur expansion resulted in their ejecting into the forbidding dinosaurian age a small group of highly modified synapsid offspring who specialized in tiny size and nocturnal habits. Selective pressures on these little creatures included an increased need to eat fast, for small size and nocturnalism leave an animal vulnerable to cold unless he eats enough to compensate with the heat of his internal furnaces. The additional increasing stresses on the jaws of these little insect-eaters resulted in the gradual appearance of the aforementioned dentary-squamosal joint, in which a single stout lower jawbone is connected to the skull through a solidly embedded cheekbone hinge for efficient and powerful chewing. By permitting food to be broken quickly into tiny pieces, thus increasing its total surface area, this arrangement makes greater amounts of food energy available to its possessors in shorter amounts of time. This in turn permits small animals to heat themselves efficiently, and, as we have seen, internal heating implies body insulation—in this case, fur. Thus, in choosing to establish the beginning of the mammalian class by reference to such jaw hinges, paleontologists locate the general span of evolutionary history in which furry "warm-bloodedness" appeared among our ancestors.

Here we are at the level of the first mammals, somewhere around 200,000,000 years ago. They were small, shrewlike beings whose life-styles were to undergo yet another 140,000,000 or so years of dinosaur-induced oppression and genetic molding before they were able to emerge from their darksome nocturnal econiches to inherit the earth. During most of this time, called the Mesozoic ("Era of the Middle Animals"), our mammalian ancestors were confined to forest-floor ghettos by their dinosaurian persecutors. From abundant fossil evidence, we are able to determine that many small dinosaurs were well suited to preying on the mammals of their time, none of which was much larger than a housecat. Such mammal-hunting dinosaurs ran

An early mammal, life-sized, of the sort that shared the world of the dinosaurs. With acute nose, mobile ears, and sensitive whiskers, such mammals found their way about under cover of night, thus evading predatory dinosaurs.

---

lightly on long birdlike hind legs and sported taloned "hands" with which they seized their prey. Judging from the shape of their skulls, we may guess that these little dinosaurs were sharp-eyed, like their living relatives, the birds; in addition, they were probably equipped with an acute sense of hearing.

The ever-active eyes and ears of predatory dinosaurs forced on our forebears a specialization in invisibility and a love of—and need for—darkness. The sense of sight being almost useless in such circumstances, these pioneering mammals "replaced" it with an enhanced dependence on the senses of smell and hearing that ultimately resulted in the remodeling of their very brains and set the stage for the emergence of mammalian self-awareness as we know it today. It was the nose in those tiny furbearers that distinguished most entities in their world, from edible insects to deadly dinosaurs; molecules reaching this nose activated sensors that sent nerve impulses to the smell centers of the forebrain. Here, these impulses were assigned responses appropriate to their sources, rather as is done in other vertebrates possessing a good sense of smell.

At this point, however, the primitive mammals departed from the vertebrate standard. There is a disadvantage in living by one's nose, especially if one is a chaser of such quick prey as insects. In bridging the distance between the smell of a fast-moving insect and that insect itself, early mammals were forced to cross gaps in both space and time—smell, in other words, is an indirect sense. Profound modifications in the cerebrum, originally a forebrain center for odor analysis, were necessary in order to cope with the new problem. Consequently we are able to trace in mammals a gradual enlargement of areas of odor association to produce a neopallium ("new cloak") on the upper surface of the forebrain's smell centers as aeons of snuffling around in the dark began to tell on the mammalian line. The neopallium became an analogue of the invisible outer world, a sort of "inner space" in which models of the real dimensions of time and space might be constructed from data received through the ever-active nose.

Peopled by "images" reconstructed from odors, the neopallial "space" was additionally delineated—given dimensions, as it were—by sounds collected from the dark surroundings through pinnae, the outer earflaps peculiar to mammals. These appendages, acting rather like radar screens in concentrating faint sounds, were (and, in canids and most other land mammals remain) movable and served to triangulate on and thus more or less pinpoint invisible sources of sound in space. Information so gathered by the ears might then be correlated in the "inner space" of the neopallium, whose importance to the early mammals was thus augmented as time went on.

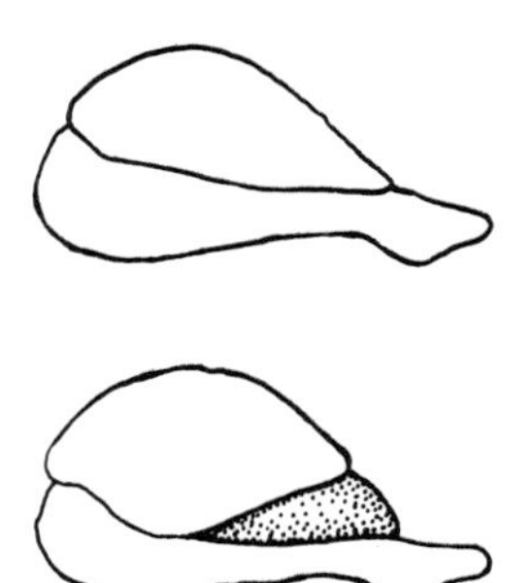

Diagrams of the cerebra of a reptile (*above*) and a mammal; the shaded area in the latter represents the neopallium in its original form.

In retrospect, the neopallium might be said to be *the* mammalian organ, since it was the chief perceptor of our essentially blind forebears' invisible surroundings. In living mammals, especially higher models such as canids, the neopallium comprises by far the largest part of the brain and is visible as the wrinkly volume that comes first to mind when we think of "brains." Here we mammals concentrate the resourcefulness of our class; here we bind time and space within an imagination born of the dinosaurian rule of the Mesozoic, a terrible time that perhaps still echoes in our "inner space," chasing the sleeping dog in his dreams and haunting, dragonlike, the human mythos.

Here our line and that of the canids diverge. During the last few tens of millions of years of the Mesozoic, at the height of the dinosaur rule, a primitive branch of the primordial insect-eating mammalian line took to the treetops in an attempt to escape the attentions of their birdlike overlords. These, the first primates, thus escaped dinosaurian dominion to emerge from the night into daylight well before most other mammals; in primates, consequently, the nose has gradually lost much of its sensory significance in daily life, to be replaced by the eyes and the sense of sight.

Primates, therefore, are heirs to a splendid color vision born of the treetop life; their eyes tend to sit prominently at the front of their faces in order better to gauge the all-important distances over which they so often leap from branch to branch high above the ground. Similarly, the style of primate life reduces their need to locate small sounds close up; their ears became receptors of social information as this task devolved from their noses, and the ear pinnae of higher primates like ourselves are consequently relatively flat

The pinnae of mammals evolved as important collectors of sound in the Mesozoic night. In modern canids such as the fennec fox shown here, these pinnae are large and handsome, serving not only to locate the sources of small sounds but also as signalers of mood and, in the case of these desert dwellers, as radiators of excess heat.

and immobile (consider, in this light, our amusement at those talented human beings who are still able to wiggle their ears). Still, primates depend on their neopallia for understanding of the world, and the shortening of their noses and ears has in no way impeded the progressive enlargement of primate neopallia to cope with their omnivorous and highly social ways.

Canids, on the other hand, retain the impoverished color perception of our common darkness-haunting Mesozoic ancestors. Dogs see a world of shades of gray, green, and brown whose details are distinguishable primarily by an acute sense of smell. In the family of dogs, therefore, the nose remains comparatively long and richly endowed with sensory epithelia with which all manner of information may be detected. Dogs check everything with their noses; their food, water, mates, moods, homes—all are located and identified by dogs primarily through scent, much as in the dark-time of our Mesozoic ancestors.

In canids the pinnae are large and mobile; not only are these lovely ears tremendously important in the location of such invisible prey as rodents-in-the-grass, but they have secondarily become organs of expression, conveying by their position a very good idea of the social rank and demeanor of individual dogs—serving, in short, as emotional semaphores to aid the poor canid eyesight in assessing the moods of others. Even human beings, given the slightest sense of empathy, are easily able to read the mood of almost any canid from the position of his ears, as we will see in more detail elsewhere.

Thus the mammalian mind was molded by dinosaurs, and thus about 80,000,000 years ago the primate line diverged from the original insect-eating mammalian stock to invade the treetops. Around 65,000,000 years ago the great dinosaur dynasty was ended rather suddenly and inexplicably;

with its demise we mark the end of the Mesozoic and the beginning of the Cenozoic ("Era of the New Animals"), the great age of mammals to whose sorry end we of the twentieth century are captive witnesses. All of the large terrestrial animals, with the exception of a few reptiles, had disappeared from the face of the earth, and the little mammals emerged from their forest fastnesses to find an immensely rich ecological vacuum awaiting exploitation by whatever vertebrates might exhibit the proper capabilities and grit.

Birds—dinosaur descendants—made a short-term stab at the occupation of large-animal econiches, but their forelimbs were already too specialized as wings to be used for manipulating food, while their toothless beaks were useless in the handling of any but comparatively soft foods such as meat. A spate of gigantic and horrifying Paleocene ("Old Dawn of the Recent") ground birds, therefore, soon gave way to the rapid rise of the mammals, which were fine-tuned through millions of years of dinosaurian oppression and, alone among land animals, superbly equipped for a bold expansion of forms and econiches.

During the early Cenozoic, birds temporarily invaded the large-animal econiches vacated by dinosaurs. Shown here is a two-meter-tall flightless *Diatryma* ("Terror-crane") standing over a primitive mammal of the time.

THE RISE OF THE CARNIVORES

The fossil record of the Paleocene and Eocene ("Dawn of the Recent") eras of between 65,000,000 and 40,000,000 years ago reveals a range of mammals both strange and already faintly familiar in form. Among these, of course, were some carnivores, mammals that embarked on a course of specialization in the eating of animals larger than insects (carnivory, after all, is just "bigger" insectivory), and the descendants of primitive insect-eating Mesozoic mammals were easily able to move into predatory econiches along a variety of evolutionary routes.

For a mammal, a life of terrestrial predation requires some special equipment. A mammal's most important food-processing tools, for instance, are the teeth, and any discussion of predation must largely concern the contents of the mouth. As we have seen, the first mammals were already equipped with superior chewing equipment; this included a set of teeth profoundly differentiated in purpose and arranged in a specific pattern originally designed for the shearing of food into tiny pieces. The early insectivores possessed, in both upper and lower jaws on either side of the head, three incisor teeth for cutting; one long, sharp, stabbing "canine" tooth—so called, of course, because of its great importance to our friends the Canidae; four shearing premolar teeth; and three grinding molar teeth. This arrangement is commonly expressed in a sort of dental shorthand; thus, three incisors, one canine, four premolars, and three molar teeth for the upper jaw of one side of the mouth,

---

Diagrammatic tooth sequences in an insectivore (*top*), a human being (*middle*), and a dog (*bottom*), showing how the "dental shorthand" is interpreted.

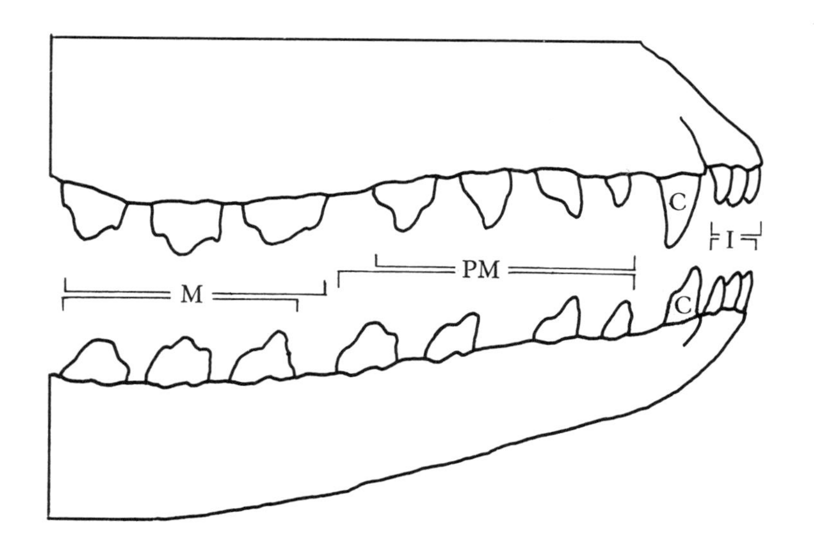

I = incisors

C = canines

PM = premolars

M = molars

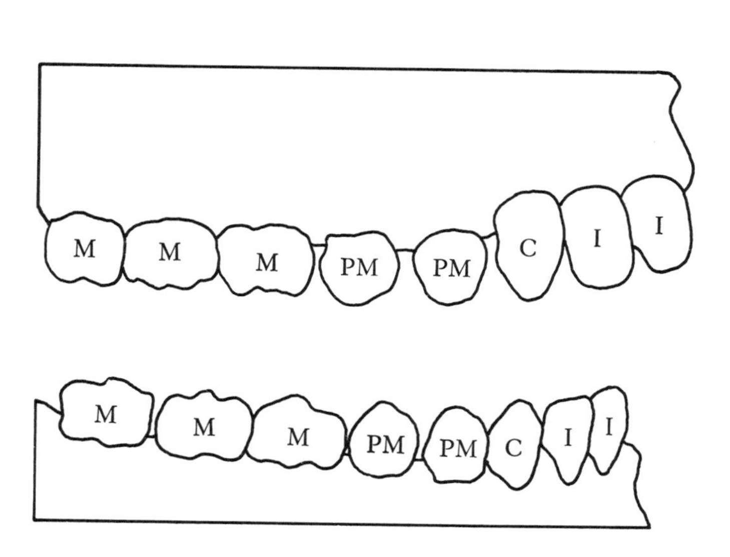

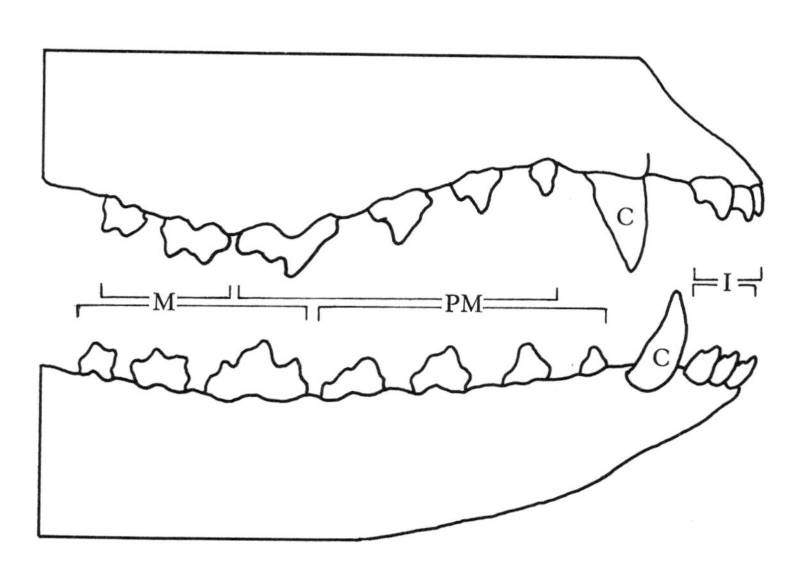

over three incisors, one canine, four premolars, and three molar teeth in the lower jaw of the same side—or 3/3 1/1 4/4 3/3, which, multiplied by two for the two sides of the mouth, produces a total of forty-four teeth in the primitive insectivores.

This is the standard arrangement, from which all the tooth specializations for different ways of higher mammalian life may be derived. We human beings, for example, are tool-using omnivores (we'll eat almost anything, but prepare it before eating with tools held in our hands); while our tools take the place of stabbing canine teeth and shearing premolars, we still retain good incisors—but only two on a side—and good grinding molars for such coarse vegetable food as we take. But we have lost two of the shearing premolars and our canines, while still there, are no longer any good for stabbing. Our dental formula is thus reduced somewhat to 2/2 1/1 2/2 3/3, for a total of thirty-two pearly whites. Similarly, the usual canid dental formula is 3/3 1/1 4/4 2/3, comprising forty-two teeth in most modern dogs; the canid formula is a more nearly complete series than ours.

In carnivorous land mammals, the incisors are still essential nippers for cutting flesh. Behind them, the aptly named canine teeth tend in such animals to be long and daggerlike, used as they are to seize and stab comparatively large prey. Carnivorous mammals are efficient eaters; except in times of unusual plenty, they are not content simply to eat the sirloin of their prey and abandon the rest. No, they eat it all, and to cope with the inevitable gristle, tough hide, and other "low-cost meats" with which they are forced to deal, mammalian carnivores need some sort of carnassial (flesh-shearing), or "knife," teeth.

Carnassial teeth have evolved independently from insectivore cheek teeth in a number of mammalian groups. Such cheek teeth were originally partially adapted to shearing, a capability that is enhanced in the evolution of carnassials by their elongation in a fore-and-aft direction, so that their blades meet one another at an angle in the manner of those of a pair of scissors. In carnivores, who need to do little grinding of their food, the molar teeth tend either to become shearers also or to disappear altogether, and thus there is often some reduction in tooth number in these animals.

Teeth, though, are only the beginning in the evolution of a carnivorous lifestyle. By definition, mammalian carnivores evolved to seek prey that is larger than an insect; in a mammalian world such as ours, this prey is primarily mammalian and, like the predators themselves, is strong and speedy. Because such prey must be chased, the toes and claws of mammalian carnivores tend to be powerful and distinct from one another, thereby offering a firm purchase on the ground (or other surface, such as tree limbs). In addition, some

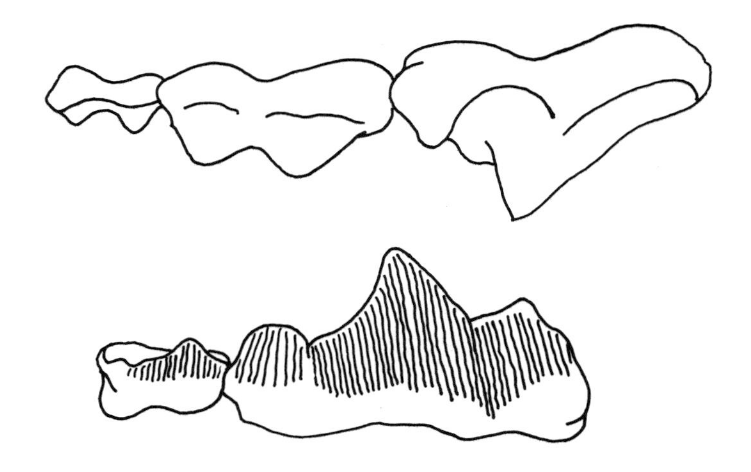

The carnassial and associated shearing teeth of a modern dog. The shading on the lower teeth delineates the surface over which the uppers slide when the mouth is closed, enabling these teeth to act like powerful scissors to cut tough fiber.

carnivores use their forefeet to aid in seizing their prey; in such cases the foreclaws may be modified to serve as grappling hooks.

Perhaps most significant of carnivore adaptations for our present consideration, however, is the mental equipment with which these mammals cope with the world around them. Because live animals, unlike vegetable food, are able to take all manner of action to stay out of predation's way, carnivores are forced to coevolve with their preferred prey if they are to eat. In the history of mammals, we find a distinct Cenozoic trend on the part of herbivores (vegetarians) to both outrun and outwit their predators in some way, or to take refuge in great size, thick skin, immense strength, or mighty herds. These defenses had to be circumvented by predators if carnivory as a way of life was to be viable; in at least the case of the living terrestrial carnivores, we find that they have done so largely by increasing their intelligence. Indeed, of all nonprimate land mammals, members of the order Carnivora—and most specifically the family Canidae—are by far the most intelligent, if by "intelligence" we mean an ability to modify one's behavior to suit changing conditions.

Intelligence is a result of efficient use of the senses, requiring of its possessor a strong capability for enhanced attention to and awareness of his surroundings. The original vertebrate land predators, such as the first synapsids, probably wandered about until they saw something to eat, and then waddled up to this prey and gobbled it down. Dinosaurs improved on this mode of hunting with better eyesight and greatly increased speed, a trend that reaches its consummation in the birds of prey with which most of us are familiar today.

Mammals, on the other hand, underwent that long period of darkness in which such a hunting mode was useless; as we have seen, they evolved in compensation an ability to hunt by tracking. When, during the Paleocene, some mammals first branched out into large-herbivore econiches, they did so already equipped with that time-binding tracking capability plus the enhanced senses of smell and hearing by means of which their ancestors had survived the dinosaurs. In hunting such animals as these new mammalian herbivores, the old walk-right-over-and-eat-'em-up mode of hunting was quite useless, mammals being, after all, the supreme Artful Dodgers.

Early mammalian carnivores, therefore, were forced to cope with such Artful Dodgers by capitalizing on the same mental and sensory advantages utilized by their prey. In place of outright mugging, modern carnivores have substituted various methods of canny stalking (requiring the ability to predict the options open to prey, and to counter these options in advance) and organized social hunting (necessitating communication of strategies for overcoming prey that by reason of strength or speed or some other defense is invulnerable to the unassisted individual predator).

Again, modern carnivores are ordinarily able to select specimens that are in some way different from their cohorts, sensing diminished fitness in these nonconformists. This tactic is especially useful in the case of herbivores that defend themselves through a herding social milieu, in which each enjoys the protection of the group's numerical superiority over predators. In preying on such animals, carnivores have evolved an ability to press the herd in some way, and then to examine it for individuals whose behavior is aberrant and which may consequently make easier prey. In this manner, precious energy is not wasted in useless attempts to catch powerful and capable animals but is put to work in more productive attacks on the defective specimens that occur in any large sampling of living beings.

As a corollary to the trend toward greater intelligence, we find that the young of carnivores are exposed to ever-increasing spans of instruction by their elders as they climb the evolutionary ladder. Education, the "leading forth" of the young, is central to mammalian success in general; in the days of Mesozoic blindness (and in the modern shrews that so closely resemble the mammals of those days) babies followed their parents about in a literal "leading forth" that served to acquaint these little animals with their invisible world before they set out on their own. With modern carnivores, such instruction takes on a new dimension; carnivores are, above all, dealers in strategy, and this art must be transmitted from one generation to the next.

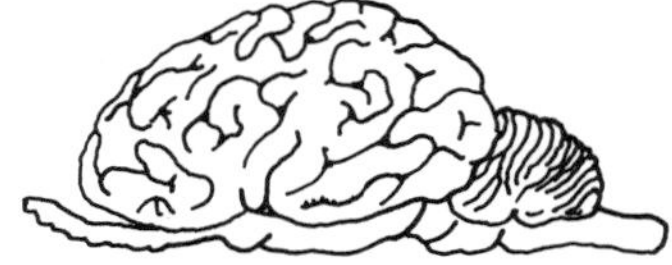
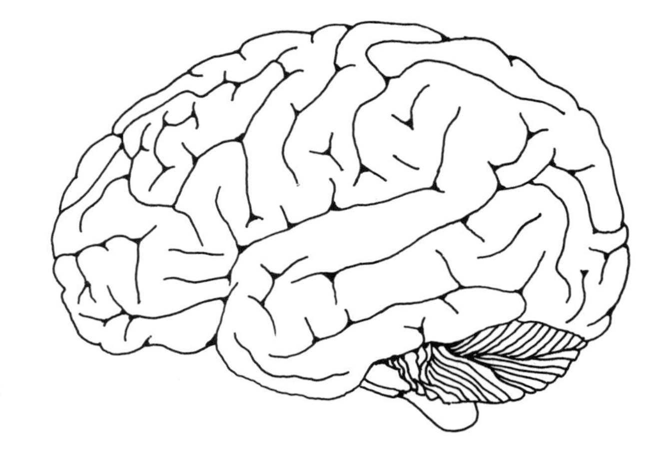

Brains of a dog (*left*) and man. In both, the convoluted neopallium is the largest portion, reflecting the high intelligence of these two mammalian species.

Complex education leads to another carnivore characteristic: the capacity for strong bonding between mothers and their young. This in turn serves as a foundation for broader social ties, such as occur between males and females within carnivore species and between assorted adults constituting packs or prides. This bonding and the complex languages evolving around it are some of the loveliest productions of the mammalian world, and throughout human history the capability of certain carnivores for loyalty and heroism among their own kind has gained the respect and admiration of people everywhere.

The culmination of such social loyalty may be found in the Canidae, with whom the hunting of prey in packs has reached its most sophisticated level among land animals (with the exception of human beings). Indeed, this loyalty has, in a distorted fashion, been extended to include human beings through the creation of the domestic dog. Dogs can display affection for us not because we are inherently lovable but because their wild wolf ancestors had such a mighty devotion for one another. The capacity for such affection is inborn, but the object of the affection may be trained into these highly intelligent and mentally malleable animals.

Yet another important social aspect of carnivory is territorialism. Because they are extremely efficient in their exploitation of prey animals, carnivores, sitting as they do at the tops of their food chains, exert considerable stress on the energy supplies available to them. Thus a prey supply tends to be divided among carnivores, whether by individual, by family, or by extended clan, in order to maximize each predator's access to prey. Such division is effected through the delineation and defense of territories by the members of a carnivore species.

There is a problem here, because carnivores are by their very nature lethally armed; among such dangerous animals any dispute over territorial rights might well result in the death of all combatants. So we find *manners* among most carnivores, manners very nearly as elaborately ritualized as those of the deadly classes of knight-warriors of medieval Europe and Japan. Ordinarily, therefore, territorial disputes within a carnivore species tend to be characterized by stereotyped signaling and mock fighting, almost dancelike in its restraint and greatly aided in its protective function by the naturally expressive and communicative natures of the participants.

The intelligence of higher carnivores is clearly apparent to anyone who has ever kept a cat or, especially, a dog. It is no accident that, of all our domesticated animals, these two carnivores most often share our houses and emotional lives; so like us are they in mind and spirit as to be well able to assimilate themselves comfortably into the complex human life-style. Intelligence, education, and communicative ability—all of these qualities are essential for most mammalian carnivores, and all reach their greatest heights among the Canidae. The story of how this came to be is one of the most interesting in the history of the mammals, and adds a good deal of depth to our understanding of the personality of *Canis familiaris*.

THE WORLD OF MAMMALIAN CARNIVORES

Our modern land carnivores, canids included, are all classed within a sub-order Fissipeda ("Split-feet," those of the order Carnivora with toes, as distinguished from the aquatic suborder Pinnipedia, the "Fin-feet," seals, walruses, and sea lions). There are some 114 living genera of carnivores, inhabiting all of the world's continents and oceans, and all of these diverse forms share a common ancestor somewhere back in the Paleocene. Carnivora, however, is not the only mammalian order to have given rise to specialist predators. During the early years of the Cenozoic Era, assorted other groups attempted to occupy the land-predator econiches, and the varying successes and failures of these groups are stories that accent the special traits granting our modern Carnivora their present monopoly of the predatory trades.

The two southern continents, Australia and South America, gave rise to a series of predatory mammals entirely distinct from the main (placental) lines of mammalian evolution. Separated from our common ancestor somewhere around 100,000,000 years ago, the marsupial mammals are distinguished from the placentals like ourselves by their possession of a comparatively primitive version of the live birth, in which the newborn young are very poorly developed and must be carried attached to teats on the outside of the mother's body before they reach the level of development of newborn placental mammals. Because of this disadvantage, marsupials never did well on the northern continents of North America, Eurasia, and Africa, early becoming extinct in these regions.

Marsupials got their big break, however, as the wandering of the continents across our planet left Australia and South America separated from the rest sometime during the late Cretaceous. (During the time of the synapsids long before, the continents had been conjoined in one great land mass, Pangaea.) It so happened that Australia and South America were initially settled by primitive marsupials, probably animals rather like the living American opossum (*Didelphis virginiana*), and it was on these isolated continents that marsupials entered the Cenozoic and diversified to occupy the various econiches inhabited elsewhere by placentals.

Because the econiches available to larger mammals are limited in number, marsupials in their isolation closely paralleled the placental mammals elsewhere as they experienced their early Cenozoic adaptive radiation. Thus, many interesting marsupial carnivores arose to prey upon the wonderful marsupial herbivores occupying the southern continents. In South America, an entire family (Borhyaenidae) of carnivorous marsupials ranging from cat- to bear-size paralleled the northern carnivorous placentals. There were sabertoothed marsupial "tiger" borhyaenids and plenty of marsupial borhyaenid "dogs" that approximated placental canids in build and appearance (although true dogs are more closely related to us and to whales than they are to any marsupial). Being more clumsily built and less intelligent than true placental carnivores, the borhyaenids became extinct when South America

---

A thylacine, or marsupial "wolf," the pouched "dog" of Australia and Tasmania. Like many extinct marsupial carnivores of South America, the thylacine parallels true canids in form; nonetheless, its primitive build and small brain probably caused its demise with the advent to Australia of such advanced hunters as human beings and dingoes.

was reconnected with North America and invaded by placental carnivores between 3,000,000 and 4,000,000 years ago.

A similar process occurred in Australia, which until the arrival of human beings within the last 100,000 years was completely uninhabited by placental mammals except for the descendants of a few drifters in the form of bats and small rodents. Here, a variety of carnivores—including the thylacine, or marsupial "wolf," and the Tasmanian devil, Australia's answer to the wolverine—survived well into the time of the European colonization of the continent. Again, however, the invasion of placental mammals (especially human beings) has driven these interesting animals to the brink of extinction. Still, the parallels between the marsupial Australian predators and their placental counterparts is a striking example of convergent evolution (a process in which organisms of different stock that occupy similar econiches tend to evolve similar forms).

The Paleocene witnessed the rise of several experimental carnivorous groups of placental mammals as these successful animals explored their ecologic limits. Among the earliest placental predators were members of the extinct order Condylarthra ("Lumpy-joints"), a group actually more closely related to the early hoofed mammals than to any carnivores with which we are familiar. Two condylarth families, Arctocyonidae ("Bear-dogs") and Mesonychidae ("Mid-claws"), flourished in early Cenozoic time; equipped with powerful canine teeth but lacking carnassials, these predators were well enough able to kill many of their stupid, primitive herbivorous contemporaries but were nonetheless limited not only by their dental inadequacies but by their clumsy builds and small brains as well. The advent of faster and more intelligent herbivores, and consequently more efficient carnivores, saw the extinction of the weird condylarths some 40,000,000 years ago.

Taxonomists, the men and women who classify organisms into groups (taxa) according to their evolutionary histories, differ on the ordering of the order Carnivora. While some insist that the group includes only the suborders Pinnipedia and Fissipeda and their common ancestors, others would include a third suborder, Creodonta ("Flesh-teeth"), which comprises two families of primitive carnivores who made a big splash during the late Paleocene and the Eocene through their "invention" of carnassial teeth for the shearing of tough flesh. Although the matter is still far from resolved, we will follow in this book the route of the great taxonomist George Gaylord Simpson by including the creodonts with the later carnivore suborders within the order Carnivora.

Suborder Creodonta probably arose from insectivore stock somewhere during the latter end of the Mesozoic, around 70,000,000 years ago. The earliest representatives of the two creodont families were the Oxyaenidae

Condylarths: a bear-sized arctocyonid (*above*) and a dog-sized mesonychid. These primitive meat-eaters, with their clumsy builds, small brains, and lack of carnassial teeth, gradually disappeared as more advanced carnivores replaced them.

("Sharp Ones"), which appeared in the later Paleocene, around 60,000,000 years ago, and quickly diversified into a number of rather weasellike animals with short, heavy skulls ranging in size from that of a rat to that of a bear. In these animals the shearing function was handled by the upper first molar and the lower second molar; the teeth behind these carnassials tended to disappear, producing in oxyaenids a characteristically short tooth row.

The second creodont family, the Hyaenodontidae ("Hyena-teeth"), arose during the early Eocene of around 55,000,000 years ago. These were long-skulled animals whose shearing teeth were the upper second molar working against the lower third molar. The hyaenodonts occupied most of the carnivore econiches of their time, the Eocene, during which they replaced the oxyaenids and shared the size diversity of that family. Hyaenodonts were longer-limbed than their oxyaenid relatives, moved faster, and were endowed with a more efficient bite, which accounted for their greater success. One hyaenodont even survived into Pliocene times, around 12,000,000 years ago, and some possessed saberlike canine teeth adapted for piercing the tough hides of giant herbivorous mammals in the manner of the later saber-toothed cats.

Although they were more than able to shear flesh, creodonts were unable to do much grinding of their food, since the molars that would have performed this task had already been specialized toward a cutting function. Thus, creodonts were ecologically limited by an inability to deal with any food that was at all coarse or abrasive. In addition, their brains were small and their limbs rather clumsily designed. Therefore, having exerted pressure on contemporary herbivores to become ever cleverer and faster, creodonts were left further and further behind. The end of the Eocene, around 40,000,000 years ago, saw the rise of more modern herbivores, especially hoofed mammals of the deer and horse orders, rodents, and lagomorphs (rabbits and their kin). The appearance of these advanced herbivores opened a vast econiche for any carnivores with the brains and speed and teeth to catch them.

Such carnivores finally arose among a family Miacidae that marks the founding of the modern carnivores. Miacids were small, lithe, tree-dwelling animals with comparatively large brains and with shearing teeth located more forward in the mouth than were those of creodonts. In miacids—and in all subsequent carnivore families including the canids—the upper fourth premolar shears against the lower first molar. The remaining molars may either be additional shearers (as in cats) or may serve, especially in more doglike carnivores, as grinders for vegetable food, permitting a measure of omnivory. Another important advantage to miacids in evolving this sort of carnassial

A bear-sized hyaenodont creodont carnivore and its skull, showing carnassial molars (shaded). Like the condylarths before them, creodonts were gradually replaced by the smarter, more agile carnivores of modern type.

---

pair was that the forward location of shearing teeth enabled comparatively young animals to use their powerful adult carnassials before all their deciduous (baby, or milk) teeth had been replaced, giving them a jump on their creodont predecessors when it came to tough foods; in prior forms the adult shearing function had to await the coming of the molars, the last of the adult teeth to appear.

Miacids appeared along with certain primitive squirrellike rodents, on which they probably preyed. With this coevolutionary trend in mind, we may guess that the miacids possessed another advanced carnivore characteristic in their killing technique, which is continued in the living carnivores and which consists of a biting attack to the head or neck of active prey—the fore end of the central nervous system—resulting in a quick kill or at least a hold that prevents retaliatory biting on the part of the captive animal. Combined with rapid shaking of the prey (the terrier shaking the rat, as an example), this sort of attack resulted in a superiority over creodonts that is reflected in the extreme flexibility and agility of miacid build.

Such a method of attack lives on essentially unchanged among modern viverrids (mongooses, linsangs, genets, and their allies), which, indeed, are so like the ancestral miacids that these two carnivore families could be linked in a single superfamily. In fact, this attack is called the "viverrid kill," and, while shared by such higher carnivores as domestic dogs and cats, it reflects the long-lost time when the miacids spawned the logical ecologic and evolutionary responses to the rise of advanced vegetarian mammals. With their slinky build, more efficient dentition, and greater smarts, miacids lie at the fork of the carnivore family tree from which the two great fissiped superfamilies, Aeluroidea ("Catlike Ones") and Canoidea ("Doglike Ones"), took their separate evolutionary paths.

Miacis, an ancestral carnivore from whose close relatives all of the living Carnivora descend. Its skull shows the modern arrangement of carnassial teeth (shaded) to which the order Carnivora owes much of its original success. Miacids looked and probably lived much as do modern viverrids such as linsangs and genets.

While some taxonomists disagree about the naming of these two superfamilies, most will agree that their divergence occurred in response to two broad sets of econiches available to carnivores at the end of the Eocene. While canoids seem to have originated as inhabitants of open grasslands, the aeluroids tended originally to be creatures of woodlands, in which the best hunting technique involved a lot of sneaking and stalking. Hence, in the three aeluroid families—Viverridae, Hyaenidae, and Felidae (cats)—the body markings usually reflect, in patterns of spotting and striping, the dappling of woodland light. As another legacy of their original habitat, the aeluroids retain (with a few significant exceptions) the solitary stalking behavior of their miacid ancestors. Thus, most of them rely on concealment and stealth to approach prey, and on a quick dash or pounce to seize it. This method attains its greatest perfection in the cats, most specialized of carnivores.

THE RISE OF THE CANIDAE

While the Catlike Ones embarked on an evolutionary voyage toward perfect (exclusive) carnivory, the Doglike Ones of the superfamily Canoidea evolved in a direction that would permit them a wider selection of the food options available from the world's ecosystems. Typical of the superfamily is an ability to survive by eating various vegetable foods in addition to flesh, and a few are even secondarily specialized to primarily vegetarian existences. This capability for omnivory offers a tremendous advantage to its practitioners, in that canoids are much less vulnerable than the Catlike Ones to changes in the population density of their prey species—themselves herbivorous animals whose numbers may vary considerably as the condition of vegetation improves or declines through the seasons and years. In hard times, when prey animals are scarce, canoids are able to drop down from the predatory top of the food chain to exploit precisely the vegetation that forms the fundament of the ecosystem; in this way an impoverished food chain can support comparatively large numbers of canoids, while their catlike relatives starve for lack of prey.

The canoid advantage is reflected in modern times by the gradual reduction in numbers of wild cats in areas settled by human beings; with the advance of industrial civilization in North America, for example, we see ever fewer wild cats such as the puma (*Felis concolor*) and bobcat (*Lynx rufus*) with the supplanting of their natural prey by domesticated stock and the restriction of their ranges by croplands. On the other hand, wild canoids such as raccoons, foxes, and coyotes are doing very well in ecosystems influenced by humanity; each of these species, able to survive on a diet of fruits and grains as well as meat, has increased its range and numbers even though most North American wildlife is reduced in numbers and regulated by human activity. As an imperfect carnivore, in short, the wild canoid is not rigidly tied

A carnivore family tree.

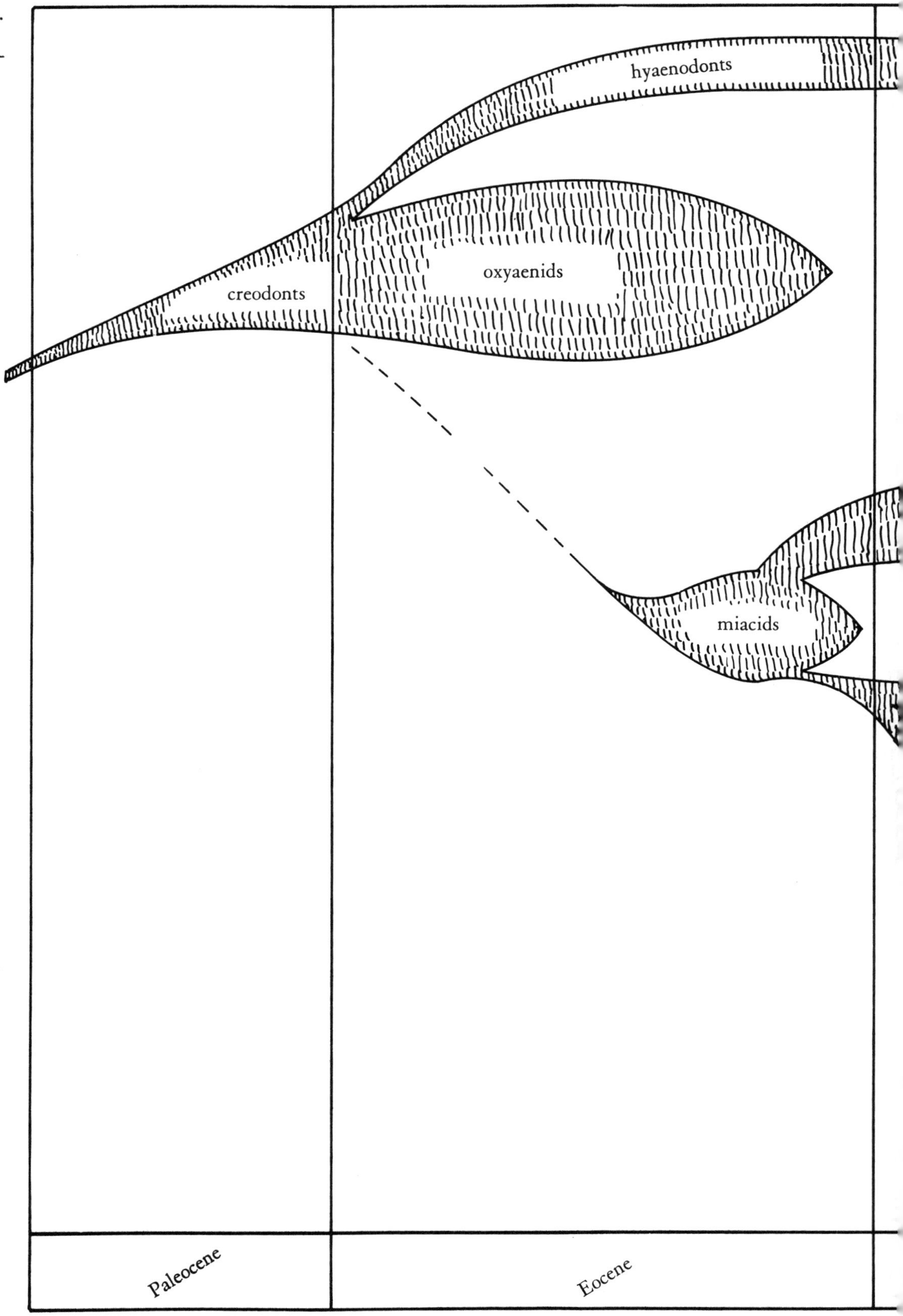

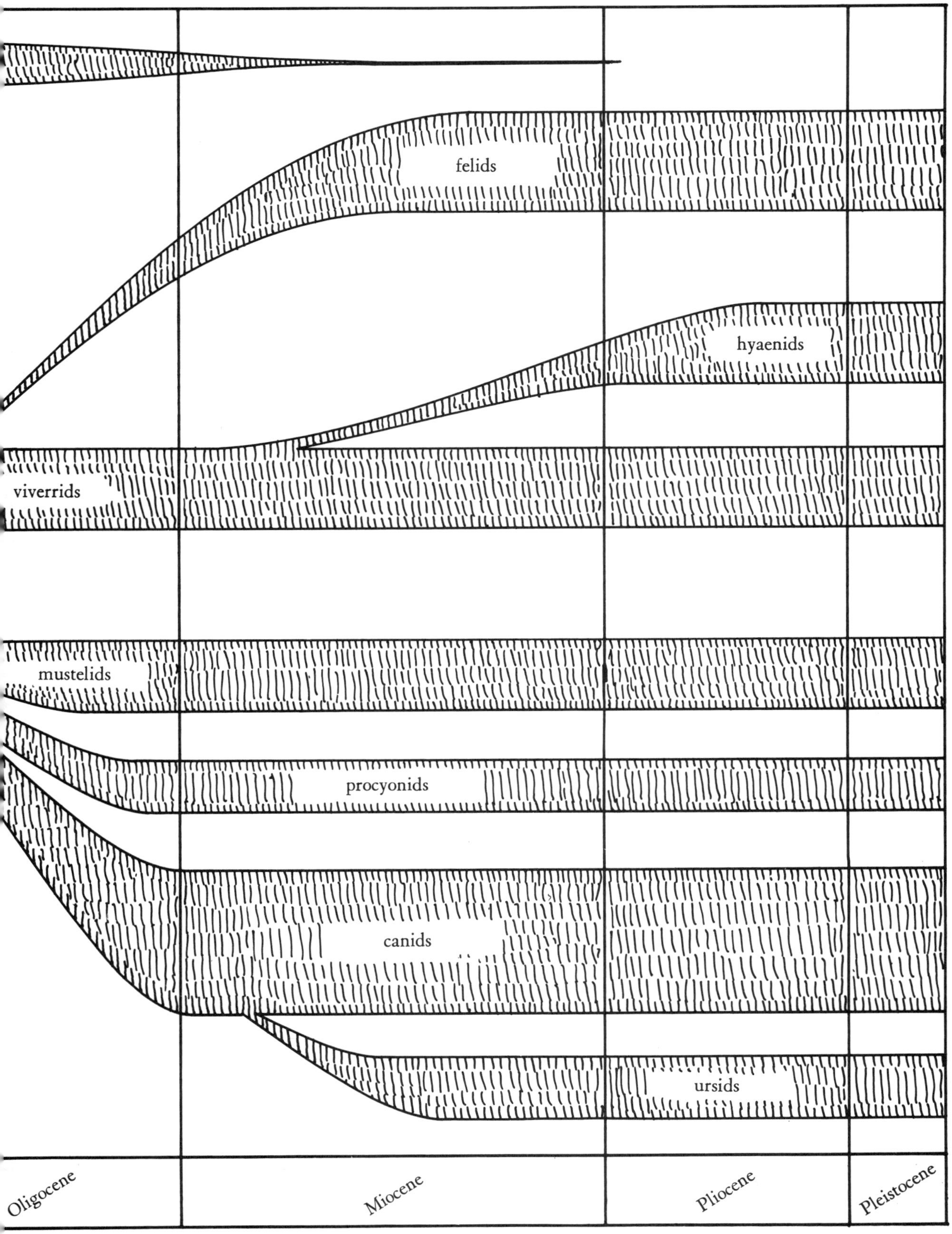

felids

hyaenids

viverrids

mustelids

procyonids

canids

ursids

Oligocene

Miocene

Pliocene

Pleistocene

to the conditions of any one food-chain position and very nearly approaches *Homo sapiens* himself in dietary adaptability.

Taxonomists, linking the canoid families on a formalized technical level, describe the superfamily Canoidea as that assemblage of Carnivora in which the auditory bullae (chambers of bone enclosing the mechanisms of the inner ear) are formed by a single tympanic bone (which encloses the eardrum in all mammals) rather than by a two-part shell as in the more catlike carnivores. Apart from auditory bullae and tympanic bones, the four canoid families—Mustelidae, Procyonidae, Ursidae, and Canidae—are immediately recognizable by anyone with a casual interest in animals. Their great success is visible in their extreme range in size, from the smallest, the American least weasel (*Mustela rixosa*)—which is only 20 centimeters long and weighs about ¼ kilogram—to the largest, the great Holarctic brown bear (*Ursus arctos*)—which weighs up to 300 kilograms and is often 3 meters tall when standing on its hind legs.

Most primitive of the four canoid clans is the family Mustelidae of weasels and their kind. In many respects little removed from their miacid ancestry, weasels are supple and low-slung in the manner of most comparatively primitive mammals; most specialized to meat-eating of the entire canoid superfamily, weasels and their kin also tend to inhabit restricted econiches—treetops, burrows, or water—rather than enjoying the wide-ranging habitats of the more advanced members of the canoid group. Moreover, most weasels are nocturnal in the manner of primitive mammals at large, having long ago relinquished to their more advanced relatives the open lands and diurnal habits of larger predators. Indeed, weasels may be regarded as close to the root of the canoid family tree; they seem to be an early northern expression of the way of life exhibited by miacids and the living viverrids, which latter inhabit southern Asia, Africa, and Madagascar today.

The biggest mustelids are the wolverine and glutton (*Gulo luscus*—literally, "blind glutton") of the circumpolar regions of Eurasia and North America; these big weasels are creatures of remote wilderness fastnesses, where they rely on strength and cunning to kill and eat almost any animals with which they share their econiches. Even the mighty bears steer clear of wolverines, and their only significant enemies are human beings equipped with firearms. Valued for their luxuriant fur and ill-equipped to coexist with

---

A weasel sampler, showing mustelid invasion of burrowing (badger, *above*), marine (sea otter, *middle*), and arboreal (marten, *below*) econiches; all nonetheless retain the typical low-slung weasel physique.

humankind, wolverines are on the run and will probably soon become extinct in all but those lands most inhospitable to human beings.

More familiar mustelids are the smaller weasels, including ferrets (long ago domesticated by Europeans as mousers), polecats, skunks, minks, fishers, and martens. The burrowing badgers and the aquatic otters are also mustelids, and it is likely that from some otterlike ancestor descended the Pinnipedia, the suborder of seals, sea lions, and walruses representing the oceanic branch of the modern Carnivora. Hunting rather in the fashion of viverrids and small cats, weasels are well known for their unique brand of almost automatic killing: once the hunt-kill sequence of activity is set in motion, a weasel may kill and kill and kill beyond its immediate needs, and so has earned a special bloodthirsty niche in the world of human folklore.

Likely descended from weasellike ancestors are all the rest of the Canoidea, the most primitive living representatives of which are the members of the family Procyonidae. Procyonid means "before-doglike," a name referring to this clan's similarity to both dogs and bears. Long ago, procyonids inhabited all of Eurasia and North America; today, two groups, Asian and American, are divided in range by the Pacific Ocean. All procyonids are plantigrade—that is, they walk on the full soles of their feet like human beings and most physically primitive mammals. Most of them spend much time in trees and are good climbers. Procyonids are typically vegetarian in habit, possessing molar teeth that are flattened at the top for grinding of coarse food. Indeed, one species, the giant panda of China, is totally specialized to the consumption of bamboo shoots.

Most familiar of procyonids to readers of this book is probably the raccoon (*Procyon lotor*, "Before-dog Who Washes His Food"), the intelligent masked omnivore of North American streamside brushlands and woods. A South American variant, the crab-eating raccoon (*P. cancrivorous*), extends the range of these beasts throughout the Western Hemisphere, where all of them coexist profitably with human beings. In keeping with their typical canoid adaptability, raccoons eat almost anything; concentrating on wild berries and other fruits, they also hunt fish and invade cornfields when the ears of corn are at their best. Other American procyonids include the ring-tailed cat, or cacomistle (*Bassariscus astutus*), the little rodent-hunter of the American Southwest and Mexico; and the weird coatis, social procyonids who move in large troops like monkeys. The coatis, which comprise three species of the

---

A procyonid sampler, showing social (coati, *above*), vegetarian (giant panda, *middle*), and rodent-eating (ring-tailed cat, *below*) forms.

genus *Nasua* ("Nosy"), come equipped with powerful hoglike noses with which they dig in an amusing manner for roots and grubs in the ground. Most completely arboreal of the procyonids are the kinkajous of South and Central American jungles, fruit-eaters who rarely touch ground throughout their lives.

From an animal very like a procyonid descended both of the remaining canoid families, the dogs proper and the bears of the family Ursidae. Like their more primitive canoid relatives among the procyonids and weasels, the bears are flatfooted, plantigrade walkers; like procyonids, they are omnivores with a marked preference for vegetation. So strong is this inclination, in fact, that alone among carnivores, bears have secondarily lost the shearing function of their carnassial teeth. Rarely do bears kill prey, with the exception of the specialized polar bears, the only total carnivores in the lot; indeed, the only killing done by most bears occurs when they fish in streams, like raccoons.

Bears and dogs diverged at about the same time from the rest of the canoid stock. Characteristically large, bears represent that branch of the superfamily that early specialized in pure size and power for personal defense; thus, these animals were able to abandon hunting for the easier, herbivorous way of life in which most of them are comfortable. It seems that bears represent a sort of "wood dog" stock, for almost all bears—again, with the exception of the polar bear—inhabit forested regions. Still, the bear and dog are very similar in physical structure, as befits forms that are so closely related, and the differences between them mainly concern diet and speed capability; bears, being so large and powerful, and so much inclined toward vegetable food, have little need for powers of running, hence their retention of the flatfooted mode of walking.

Which brings us to the last canoid family, the Canidae, the true "Dogs" with which the rest of this book deals. These, the most specialized of the canoid superfamily for active seeking of speedy prey, are the only digitigrade (toe-walking) sprinters of the lot. In all canids, the feet are elongated in the region of the "wrist" or "instep," so that effectively a third segment is added for faster and more energy-efficient running than is possible for flatfooted animals such as weasels, raccoons, or bears. With the toe-walking gait comes bluntness of claws, so that canids no longer use their "hands" in capturing their prey or manipulating food, as do their more primitive relatives; instead,

---

An ursid sampler, showing a brown bear and its skull, with flat molars adapted for a largely vegetarian diet (*above*); a polar bear, most carnivorous of the family (*below, right*); and a Malay sun bear (*below, left*), whose diet consists largely of insects and honey.

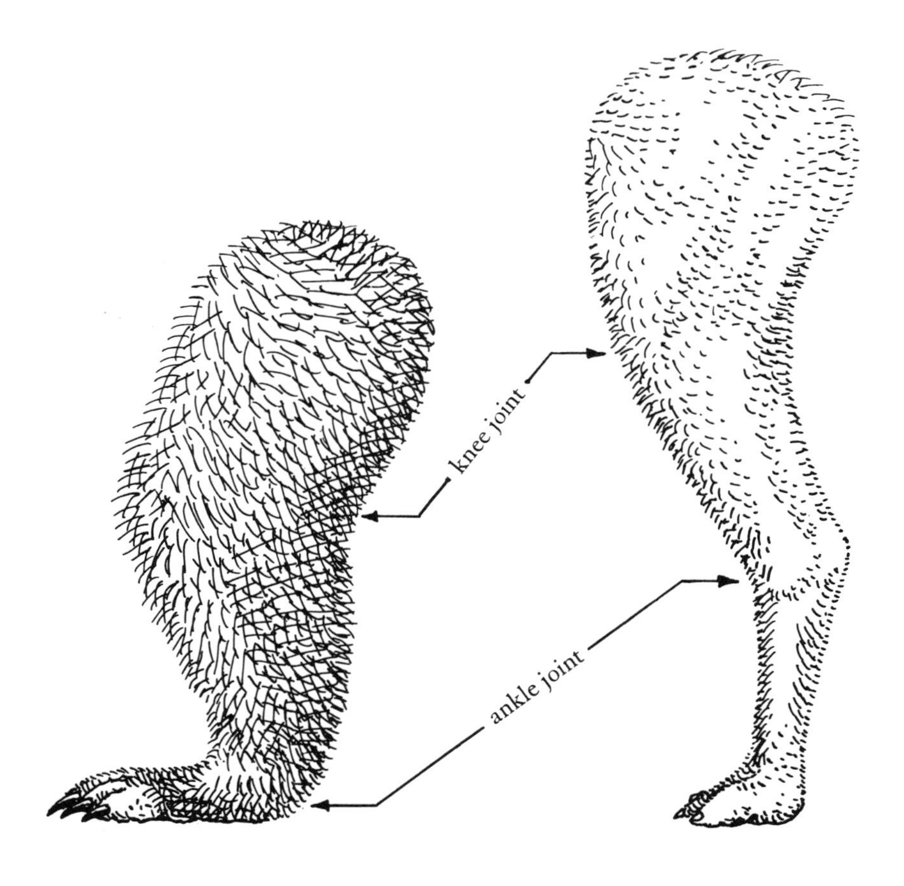

Plantigrade (*left*) and digitigrade hind legs of a bear and a dog, respectively, showing the lengthening of the canid foot for faster running.

---

this function is entirely relegated to the jaws, which are characteristically long and constitute that "dog look" common to all members of the family.

Family Canidae expresses in form and function an ancestral invasion of open country wherein prey must be hunted by tireless running rather than by stalking. In the act of this invasion, the ancestral canids also abandoned much of the fruit-eating life-style of procyonids and bears for more specialized dining on active herbivores captured in the chase. In fact, the rise of long-legged digitigrade herbivores such as horses, antelope, deer, goats, and wild cattle coincided with that of canids, for it was their interaction on the plains and grasslands that resulted in high-velocity mammals as a whole. The wolf is father to the deer—which, in turn, is father to the wolf.

Taxonomists recognize a complex of characteristics strictly delineating the Canidae among their more broadly canoid relatives; all of these characteristics are directly derived from the cursorial (running) way of life, and together they produce a physiology of endurance unmatched in other mammals. Most obvious, of course, is the structure of the canid leg, in which certain bony elements are fused to produce a stronger unit for galloping tirelessly after prey. Alone among carnivores, canids have a reduced number of hind toes (four)—the Cape hunting dog of Africa carries this specialization further with the loss of a foretoe as well.

Additionally, the body-cooling system is highly advanced in canids, enabling these runners to keep going without danger of overheating on even the hottest of days. Cooling in canids, like that in human beings, is based on the evaporation of water from moist body surfaces that are richly supplied with blood vessels. In human beings, cooling is largely accomplished by sweating and the consequent evaporation of moisture from the skin; in canids the same evaporative process is accomplished throughout the surfaces of the respiratory system in the activity we call panting. Panting is not connected with respiration (oxygenation of the blood) per se; it is a specialized activity in which the breathing rate increases, not in response to carbon dioxide levels in the blood but in response to the temperature of the body as a whole. In other words, a cool but galloping dog will breathe harder in order to oxygenate his blood, while a warm dog, even at rest, pants—but only to cool that blood by passing it around and through the respiratory system at a rapid rate. Not only is the blood cooled as it passes through the lungs; in canids the long nose contains some fifteen times the sensory area of that of human beings, and throughout its extent this area is supplied with blood vessels. A network of blood vessels at the base of the canid brain, called the *rete mirabile* (literally, "miraculous net"), carries blood cooled in the nasal passages across hot blood rising from the heart toward the brain; in this manner the blood entering the brain is cooled by conduction of its excess heat to the nasally cooled blood and an even temperature is maintained in that all-important organ.

Location of skin glands producing odors for communication in canids; the supracaudal (tail), anal, and interdigital (foot) glands are shaded.

Connected with the large area of the nasal epithelia (linings) in canids is their superb sense of smell. Like the primordial mammals, and unlike primates such as human beings, canids depend to a great extent on odors to locate prey and to communicate with one another. As auxiliary aspects of this mode of communication, a set of body glands is distributed about the canid individual for production of odors—pheromones—used in social interaction. Between the pads of the feet, glandular pockets set scents to trails, so that one canid of a social group may easily follow another within hours or even days after the first passed by. At the top of the base of the tail, the supracaudal gland (called in foxes the "violet" gland, for its distinctive odor) offers information on the sexual status of a canid, while other glands alongside the

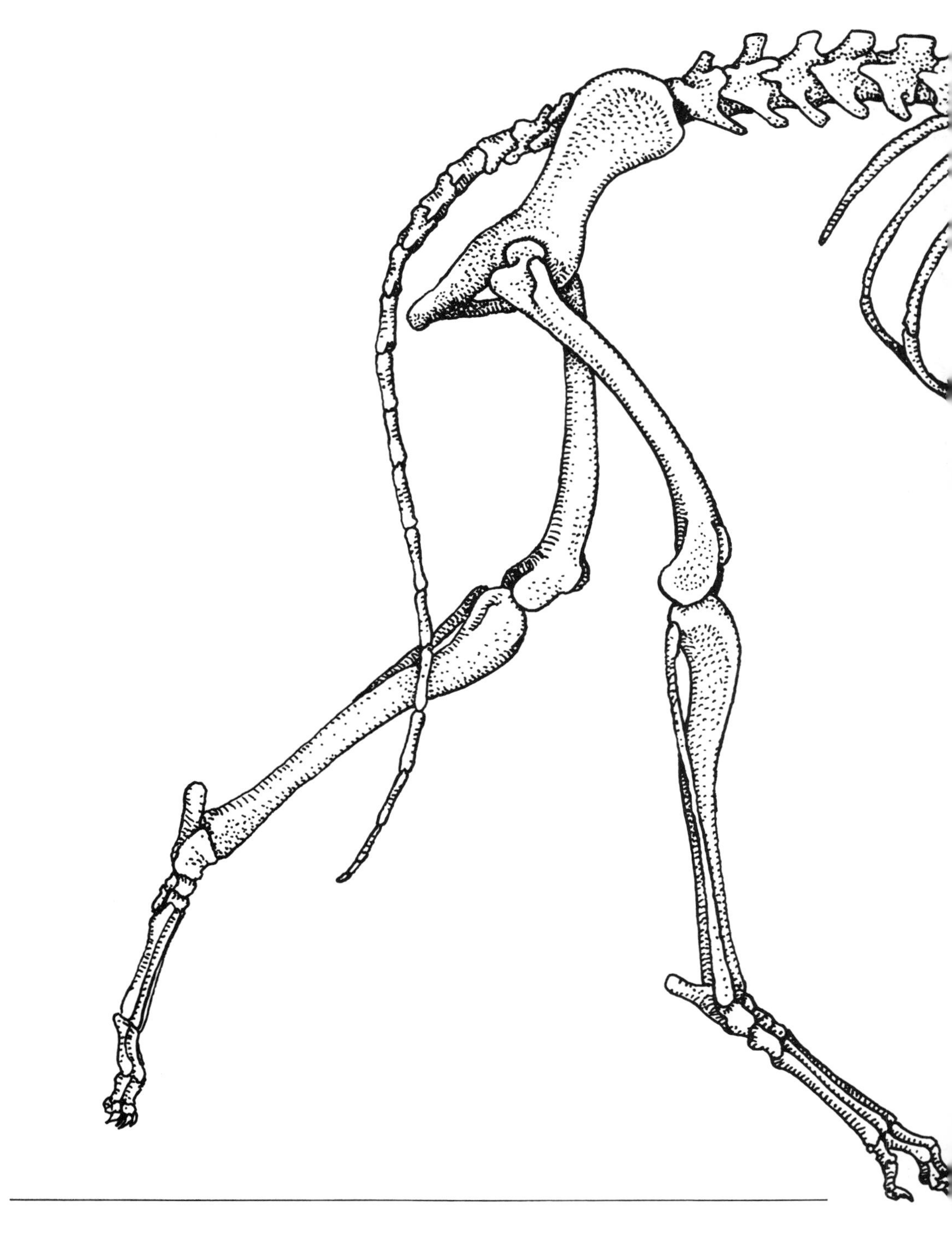

The canid skeleton (in this case, that of a wolf) is a graceful structure reflecting millions of years of selection for tireless running across open land in pursuit of prey.

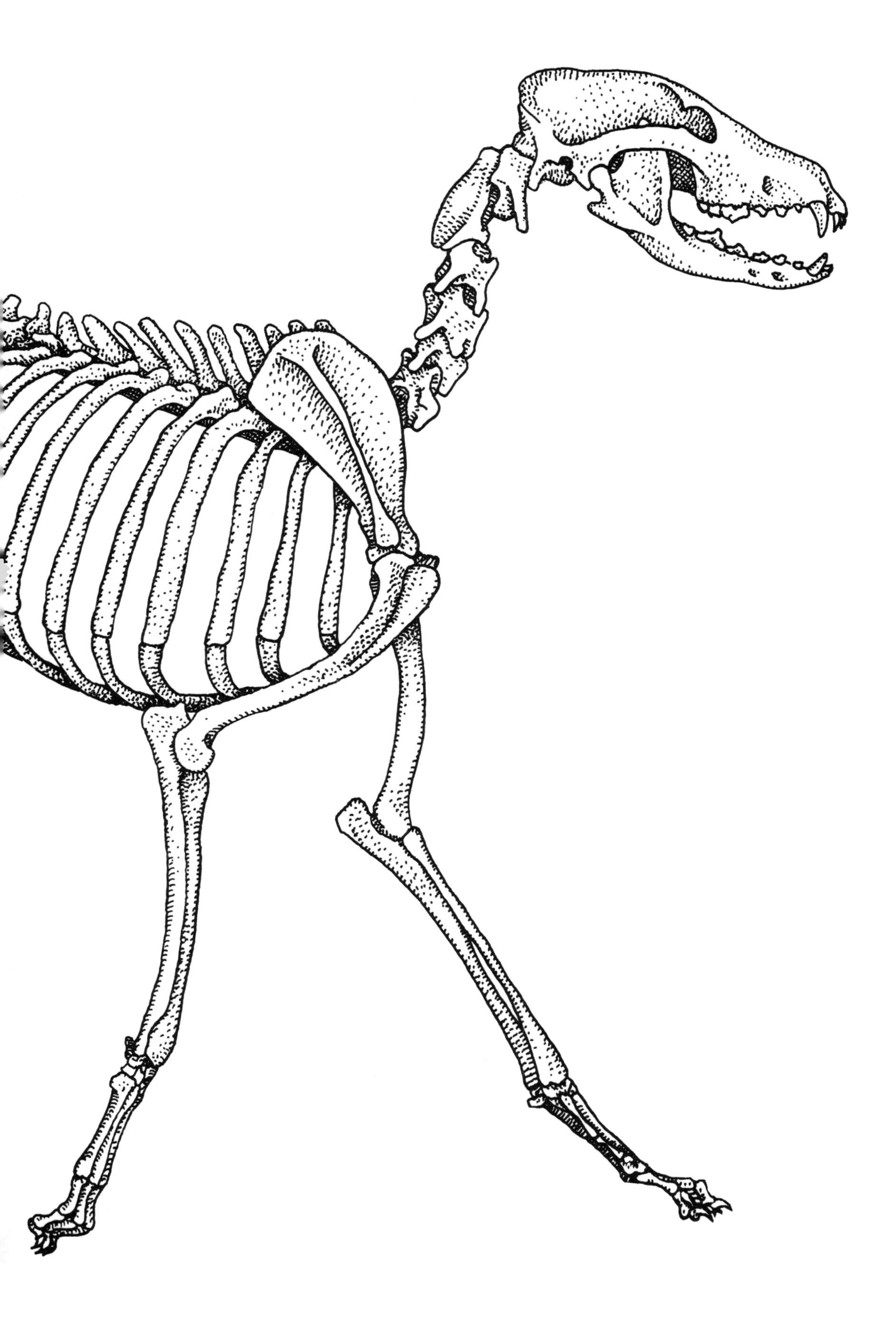

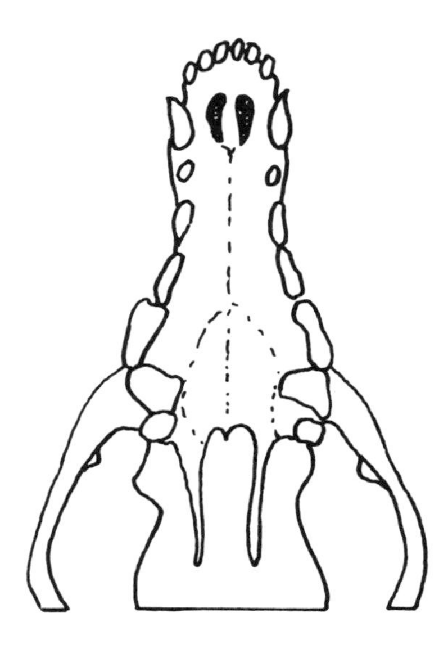

Dog in *Flehmen* (*left*), and diagram showing location of Jacobson's organs in roof of mouth between canine teeth.

---

anus mark a canid's feces for the "reading" convenience of others. Canid urine, too, contains a wealth of information readable by the acute noses of others of the kind; an individual's identity, age, sex, and mood may all be identified by other canids through urinary analysis by nose, and all canids therefore mark the boundaries of their territories, their preferred paths, and, indeed, all of their wanderings by the use of urine on conspicuous landmarks.

The mighty sense of smell in canids may be illustrated by the fact, experimentally shown, that a dog can detect the scent of a human fingerprint some six weeks after the trace was laid. It is this acuteness of smell that permits one wild canid to detect, for example, the odor of fear in the urine of another which has long since passed by, and thus to be on the lookout for trouble in advance. Canids are aided in their sense of smell by a pair of small openings, Jacobson's organs, in the front of the roof of the mouth. Using these, a canid "tastes" the air as he smells it, curling his lips to do so in a motion referred to by the German word *Flehmen.* In *Flehmen,* the animal raises his nose, wrinkles his snout, and ceases breathing while he bares his fore-teeth and samples the air with his Jacobson's organs. *Flehmen* may be observed in any dog testing a urinary scentpost, and produces a sort of silly smile characteristic of this sort of canine newspaper-reading.

The fossil record offers fragmentary traces of canids as far back as 35,000,000 years ago in the bones of such coyote-sized animals as the "Half-dog" *Mesocyon.* Long-bodied and short-limbed, *Mesocyon* nevertheless shows a strong relationship to procyonids and bears; however, his leg structure shows him already to have been experimenting with the cursorial life-style that would characterize all of his living canid descendants. With this life-style came the abandonment of stealth-hunting in favor of the more direct attack, and with this form of attack came a new predatory opportunity—that of hunting in groups. Because to be successful the stalking method requires a hunter to work alone, the potential size of his prey is sharply limited. Cats, for instance, rarely pursue anything larger than themselves because as solitary hunters they have a better chance of overpowering prey if it is their own size or smaller. In open land, where stalking is not feasible, mammalian prey also tends to be larger and more powerful than most predators. Here, social hunting, the sharing of the task by many at once, becomes very rewarding; with a little help from his friends, a predator is able to pull down animals far larger than himself, and can thus invade a food source of vast potential.

Well on the way toward a running/hunting way of life, *Mesocyon* was probably also experimenting with the social group. With this mode of hunting

---

Restoration of *Mesocyon*, a primitive canid. The body markings shown here, while conjectural, are likely similar to the patterns from which social-signaling markings (dark ear tips and manes erected in dominance displays, white facial patterns to guide ritual muzzle biting, and so on) are derived in modern canids from the more primitive forest-dwelling carnivores.

comes a need to communicate within the pack on a level more sophisticated than that of mere odor; in canids this interaction is aided by a strong and variable voice embracing a range of squeaks, yips, barks, growls, and drawn-out ululating howls seldom equaled among other animals of any sort. Also, almost all canids also show a set of conspicuous body markings by which an individual may convey a sense of his mood to any nearby canid (or human) observer. The "semaphore" system of ear and tail movements, for instance, is aided by strongly delineated markings on these appendages to aid the poor canid eyesight in their "reading," and the more sociably inclined canids share in the possession of manes of long hairs, darker than the rest of the body, which are erected as a sign of dominance or anger. The face, long-snouted and broad, is also equipped with various markings to aid in the reading of its movements. The jaws tend to be surrounded with lighter fur, probably signalling movements associated with the friendly ritual nip and mutual grooming, and a ruff about the face as a whole is raised to enlarge the canid aspect in times of rage. As the progenitor of the canid way of life, *Mesocyon* probably possessed many of these markings in a generalized form, so that his restoration on page 000 may best be used to illustrate them.

From old *Mesocyon* or someone very like him descended a variety of very impressive canids of giant size, a sideline of the family often called "bear-dogs." Flourishing between 30,000,000 and 3,500,000 years ago, bear-dogs such as *Amphicyon* ("Part-dog") were canine forms experimenting with a partly herbivorous, bearlike life-style, attesting to the canid ability to return to vegetarianism when conditions force them to do so. The bear-dogs were replaced by true bears of the modern type, but the ability to eat vegetation survives in all canids in the form of their molars; unlike those of most other predators, canid molars remain grinders and canids are still, to a certain extent, omnivores.

Other early canids experimented with a life of perfect and exclusive carnivory like that of the cats; among these were dogs of the genus *Hesperocyon* ("Western Dog"), housecat-sized predators of great agility and grace that probably hunted small rodents and birds rather in the manner of modern foxes. The canid line also produced a variety of great hyenalike scavengers such as *Osteoborus* ("Bone-crusher") and *Simocyon* ("Short-faced Dog"). Most important to us, however, was the line that led from *Mesocyon* to the wolflike *Tomarctus*, a North American genus that founded the modern family Canidae. It was in *Tomarctus* that the fifth toe on the hind foot first appeared as a vestigial dewclaw, an adaptation reflecting an increasing dependence on rapid running as a way of life. *Tomarctus*, roaming the plains some 10,000,000 years ago, seems therefore to have established the best way of life for canids; from that point

Three extinct canids. *Hesperocyon,* the catlike "Western Dog" (*above*); *Osteoborus,* the "Bone-crusher" (*middle*); and *Tomarctus,* "Almost-a-bear," an early canid of essentially modern form (*below*). From a *Tomarctus*-like animal are descended all living canids.

onward, all the catlike, bearlike, and hyenalike dogs became increasingly rare as what we would call doglike dogs took over.

The modern family Canidae quickly diversified from its North American foundation to spread across all of the world's continents except Australia and Antarctica, both isolated from canid expansion until the coming of human beings with boats. The thirteen living genera within the family reflect its tremendous success as a carnivorous group specializing in speed and cleverness as a way of life but able to revert to vegetables as a food source should the need arise. (The entire family Felidae of cats, in contrast, includes only the three genera *Lynx*, *Felis*, and *Panthera*.) Even excepting the domestic dogs, we may confidently list family Canidae among the most successful living mammals, certainly *the* most successful of carnivores. Owing their success to brains and adaptability as well as running speed, the canids in many ways share the advantages of humans in invading new lands. As we examine the different genera of canids in succeeding chapters, their seemingly manlike character, which ultimately provided the foundation for the dog's domestication, will become ever more apparent.

REYNARD THE TRICKSTER AND OTHER FOXY TYPES

Of 285 fables of Aesop in my daughter's collection, 29, or about 10 percent, contain in their titles reference to foxes ("The Fox and the Grapes," "The Lion, the Fox, and the Stag," and so on). This figure, while not including the many fables in which foxes play a part but do not appear in the titles, suggests that of all nondomesticated animals the fox played the most significant part in the Eurasian folklore of ancient times, especially in his wonted guise as Trickster of the agricultural Europeans of north-temperate ecosystems.

The Trickster is a constant in primitive mythological traditions. Assuming the form of the cleverest animal known to a specific culture, he represents the everlasting uncertainty principle and its action on human affairs. In India and Southeast Asia, he is Monkey; in northwest North America, he is Raven; in southwest North America, he becomes Coyote, yet another tricky canid. In more advanced mythological cycles he sometimes assumes human form, notably as Loki among the Norse gods and Satan in the Christian tradition. Trickster is usually in trouble of some sort, often clownishly so, but always manages to come out on top—as does, more often than not, Reynard.

With at least 10,000,000 years of human malice operating against him, the red fox (*Vulpes vulpes*) native to Eurasia and North America has become ever more proficient at circumventing the wiles of humanity. In so doing, he has earned a large measure of grudging admiration from his human cousins—in fact, he was long ago given the unique semi-proper name Reynard (or Renard, or Regnard), which is derived from the Middle High German poem "Fuchs Reinhard" and a later version, the *Roman de Renart*, itself a delightful series of fox-trickster tales of medieval Europe.

The red fox, of course, is not the only fox. Classification of these little canids (none larger than an Airedale, many as small as housecats) is variable, depending on whose work one favors. Traditionally, the world's foxes are grouped in several genera independent of the genus *Canis*, itself reserved for the assorted true wolves and domestic dogs. Many workers, however, prefer an older system of classification that would include within *Canis* at least the Eurasian and North American foxes. Still, as we will see when we consider *Canis* itself, the point remains moot, canids being at once homogeneous and highly variable in form and habit. In deference to convenience and the fact that the number of chromosomes is different in foxes from that in dogs, I will adhere to the taxonomic form in which several genera are permitted to account for dogs and foxes.

Beginning with that old coevolver with humanity, *Vulpes vulpes*, we find one of the most naturally widespread single species of higher mammals on the planet. With a range equaled only by that of the true wolves, Reynard shares with them the dubious honor of having been one of the carnivores most intimately involved with human beings during the earliest stages of their transition from tribes of hunter-gatherers to settlers of agricultural townships. Per-

---

The red fox often stalks and pounces on rodents much in the manner of a housecat.

haps our best look at the Neolithic societies that experienced this transition is provided by the ruins at the ancient Palestinian town of Jericho. Among animal remains found here are those of at least 134 individual red foxes; in some strata these foxes outnumber all other animals. These proto-Neolithic foxes were somewhat larger than the modern ones, reflecting more easily available supplies of food in those preagricultural times; already, however, human beings were exerting pressure on their kind, hunting them both for food and for their gorgeously luxuriant fur.

We can assume that the experience at Jericho was nearly universal. At any rate, as human societies became more and more dependent on the products of their agriculture, so did red foxes; from the beginning, these little canids seem to have been significant competitors with human beings for the fruits of their labors in the fields. "Take us the foxes, the little foxes, that spoil the vines," called Solomon, but it didn't help, and with the later advent of domesticated birds and rabbits, Reynard took to investigating and often slaying these easily captured forms of his natural small prey. In so doing, of course, he brought himself ever more frequently to the attention of his human competitors.

Red foxes seem from the start to have been beautifully adapted to living among agricultural settlements. Preferring as they do the brushlands edging forests, they are at their best wherever human beings maintain fields and pasturelands dotted with forests, hedges, and scrub. Because this is the land pattern most commonly associated with agriculture in Europe and North America, the red fox native to these continents experiences a population increase whenever human beings bring previously unsettled areas under cultivation. Among the most important advantages conferred upon Reynard by farmers is probably their intolerance of other wild predators such as wolves and cats, whose econiches naturally overlap that of the fox. These others, more conspicuous or less wily predators are so often extirpated by hunting, trapping, and poisoning that their prey, in the form of rodents and birds, becomes available to foxes free of competition.

The legendary cunning of Reynard the Trickster, his uncanny ability to avoid the poisons, traps, and other stratagems arrayed against him, have a history as old as agriculture. With the replacement of its vast postglacial forests by the hedges and fields of agricultural man, Europe became in essence an artificial biome within which most of the avian and mammalian life was regulated by human activity. Human beings, classifying animals by their usefulness in human life, divided the wild denizens of their farmlands into "game" animals such as grouse and rabbits, and "vermin," those animals which competed for game and crops with humans. Reynard, lover of the flesh of birds and rabbits as well as occasional thief of fruits and vegetables,

A fox hunt, an expensive production whose complexity reflects that of the brain of Reynard.

was naturally included among the vermin and by the time of the Middle Ages was undergoing relentless persecution by peasants and feudal landholders alike.

Recalling that the red fox had undergone millennia of selection at the hands of man before this time, we can see that he was already well prepared to sustain the unwelcome attentions of humankind. Traps, poisons, arrows and, later, bullets, have done little to affect Reynard's populations; indeed, he thrives as never before throughout his former range (excluding, of course, the paved and ecologically almost sterile enclaves called cities). So proficient, in fact, is the red fox at steering clear of his would-be murderers that human beings have been forced to design special breeds of dogs (foxhounds and fox terriers) and even horses (hunters) to pursue him. The fox hunt in all its equestrian panoply reflects the simple fact that foxes have outdone man on his own—they must be pursued by entire troops of humans mounted and armed and preceded by platoons of specially bred and trained canid slaves!

With a body length of only about 60 centimeters and a tail of about half that length, the red fox is small enough to remain nearly invisible even in thickly settled areas. Foxes are light and agile, almost catlike in movement; this natural vulpine grace, coupled with their elegant coats and bearing as a whole, earn them human admiration above and beyond that for their cunning—witness, as an example, the phrase "foxy lady." Catlike, too, is Reynard's mode of hunting; he (or she—Reynarda, perhaps) is unlike most of his larger canid relatives in that he is a stealth-hunter. Hunting in packs is most effective in the pursuit of big game, of course, and in the man-dangerous world of the fox such group tactics would only attract unwanted attention. Specializing so explicitly in the killing of insects and small vertebrates, the red fox shares many of the techniques exhibited by small cats like the domestic forms, even to the point of occasionally climbing trees! Like the cat also in being a nocturnal hunter, the fox possesses elliptical pupils; these permit maximal light-collecting eyesight at night while allowing the pupils to contract to tiny slits in bright light. In all, it is strange and delightful to see in this little dog-creature all the stalk and pounce we expect of the household cat.

Unlike the cat, of course, Reynard is anything but a hyperspecialized carnivore. His molar teeth are well designed for the grinding of vegetable matter, and foxes have a distinct weakness for such delicacies as blueberries, cherries, rose hips, apples, grapes, even sour ones ("The Fox and the Grapes"), sweet corn, squashes, and melons. Red foxes, therefore, enjoy comparative immunity from changes in the food supplies of their communities, an essential advantage in the biologically impoverished surroundings of human beings.

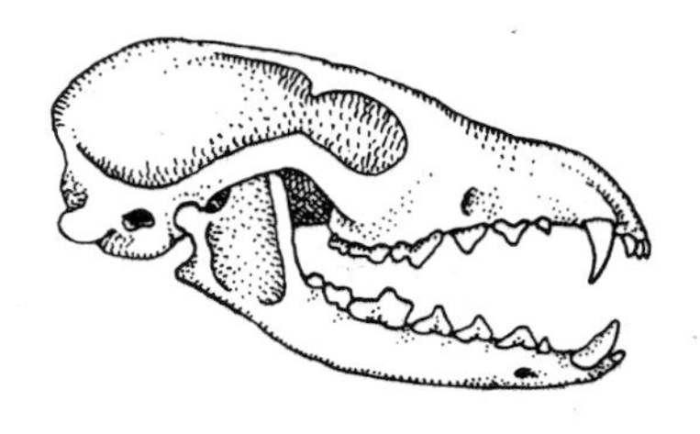

Skull of a red fox, showing molars partially adapted to grinding vegetation while the rest of the teeth are those of a typical flesh-eating canid.

Foxes mate in winter, usually around the end of January or in early February; the male is called a "dog," the female a "vixen." If undisturbed by human activity, foxes choose the same mate year after year until death do them part, so that their territories are mutually maintained by a male and a female. The pair excavates extensive systems of burrows, within which three to ten young are born in April after a gestation period of about fifty days. Diversity, of course, is a hallmark of canid evolution, and within a single litter of "red" foxes any or all of the four typical vulpine color phases may appear. These include the standard red fox; the "cross" fox, who bears over his shoulders and back a cross-shaped mane of darker hair; the melanistic, or dark, phase—black with white-tipped guard hairs; and the silver phase, lightest of all.

Both fox parents care for the young, the male initially doing the hunting while his mate remains in the den to nurse the newborns. After about a month, the youngsters occasionally emerge from the lair, then begin to spend more and more time outside as they perfect their walking and set about acquiring some of the grace characteristic of the species. After about two months, young foxes are following their parents on hunting forays; beginning with insects, the kits work upward in prey size as their prowess increases until they can catch rabbits, the biggest prey they'll ever likely take. In addition to their hunting and sampling of vegetable food, the young foxes learn with increasing age to assess carrion for its safety; foxes are inveterate scavengers, but thousands of years of sorry experience with baited traps has taught them that human beings all too often leave lethal apparatus about to snare the unwary.

By the middle of autumn, the kits have learned to eat almost anything and are spending much time away from the home den. Ultimately, they seek new hunting territories of their own, invading newly cleared areas or displacing older or infirm foxes. Youngsters may range as far as 200 kilometers in search of territory; this propensity for wandering, together with his catholic eating habits and ability to cope with humanity, has assured Reynard a wide distribution for some time to come.

Not least among the advantages conferred on red foxes by their long competition with humanity has been the lasting admiration of the latter. Thus, from their original Holarctic range (around the Arctic Circle in Eurasia and North America), they have been introduced by human beings to such far-flung regions as Australia, New Zealand, and South America. True to form, Reynard adapts superbly anywhere he is planted, even though the purpose of his transposition is mainly to provide his human hosts with sport in the hunt. Red foxes are also raised on farms for their fur, which, it must be said, loses most of its charm when transferred from its original owner to the shoulders of a heedless woman in a polluted city.

There are other foxes around the world, all of them more or less like Reynard in that they depend on small size and omnivorous habits to stay out of trouble. The North American gray fox (*V. cinereoargentatus*—literally, "gray-silver"), sometimes placed in a separate genus *Urocyon*, is a sort of timber fox of the eastern United States and Canada. Less cunning and man-wary than the red, he suffers more from the expansion of civilization but remains widespread throughout much of his original range, which extends south to Central America. Being more of a forest dweller than Reynard, the gray fox climbs trees and likes to nest in hollows far above the ground; this is a fatal predilection where clearing of timber is carried out, and in such cases the range of the gray fox suffers to the advantage of that of the red.

Another fox inhabiting the North American continent is the swift (*V. velox*, "Fast-fox") of the plains east of the Rocky Mountains from Canada to Mexico. The swift is, in keeping with its prairie habitat, a soft tawny color with a bushy, black-tipped tail. The kit, a desert subspecies, is the smallest North American fox. With a total length of only 75 centimeters, and conspicuously large ears, the kit fox represents the successful invasion by its kind of the Southwestern desert—an environment in which the total amount of useful biomass is very small. In order to maintain numbers great enough for a gene pool that will not backbreed and destroy itself, these foxes have responded to arid conditions with small size except for their prodigious ears, which act as enormous radiators of excess body heat. Both swift and kit foxes are comparatively unwary and easily trapped; unfortunately, these lovely animals are becoming increasingly rare.

In Asia and Africa the genus *Vulpes* is represented by yet other local fox forms adapted to varying climates and ecologic communities. Thus the central Asian corsac fox (*V. corsac*), the Tibetan fox (*V. ferrilatus*), the Indian desert and Bengali foxes (*V. leucopus* and *V. bengalensis*), the southwest Asian

The tree-climbing gray fox (*right*) and the tiny, big-eared American kit fox.

or Blanford's fox (*V. canus*), and the Cape silver fox of southern Africa (*V. chama*). Indeed, in all its variants the genus *Vulpes* fairly shouts the goodness and plenty of the foxy way of life.

"Fox" is a common name for small canids in general, and many such creatures of genera other than *Vulpes* have evolved to fit special places in the nature of things. In Africa, for instance, we find the bat-eared fox (*Otocyon megalotis*, "Eared Dog with Big Ears"), a unique brand of canid in that its dental formula, 3/3 1/1 4/4 4/4, places it at the very top of the land-dwelling mammalian dental line, with a total of forty-eight teeth. (Of all placental mammals, in fact, only toothed whales possess more teeth!) Sharing with the kit foxes a set of gigantic ears for heat radiation, the bat-eared fox inhabits semi-

The insectivorous bat-eared fox of Africa; his facial markings invite ritual grooming from others of his kind.

arid country in which it eats mostly insects, a crunchy diet to which it probably owes its six-tooth advantage over the rest of the canids.

Another desert fox with radiator ears is the fennec (*Fennecus zerda*) of northern Africa. Colonial in its habits, the fennec lives in small underground "towns" excavated beneath sand dunes, and emerges at night to seek its prey of insects, small reptiles, rodents, and birds. Perhaps the most completely carnivorous of foxes, the fennec is so perfectly adapted to its desert environment that it need never drink water; it obtains all it requires from its diet. Fennecs also wear "sand shoes," possessing as they do broad hairy soles of the feet on which they can run lightly over the shifting sands of their arid homelands. Their sociability makes fennecs conducive to taming, and these

The tiny fennec sports a spectacular set of radiator ears, a necessity in his Saharan habitat.

beautiful little animals have long served as companions to the various peoples who share the terrible northern Sahara with them.

From the Sahara to the Arctic Circle is a long jump, but another species of fox, the Arctic (*Alopex lagopus*), is native to the entire region of the North Pole—and nowhere else. As perfectly adapted to his frigid home as is the fennec to the Sahara, this "harefoot" fox (so called because of his snowshoe-like feet, which enable him to walk easily over snow and ice) also inhabits communal systems of burrows. In response to his harsh environment, the Arctic fox sports a gorgeous thick coat designed to keep out the relentless cold and serving secondarily as camouflage; in winter his coat is snow-white, while in summer it is a blue-gray that blends in well with snowless tundra soils. Unfortunately, this coat is also coveted by human beings. Fortunes have been made through the trapping of these foxes, which are comparatively bold and innocent of trap wisdom, and in modern times fox ranches produce tens of thousands of pelts each year for the clothing industry. I cannot over-emphasize in this context my feeling that these pelts look far better on foxes than on vixens of the human variety.

Human beings are not the Arctic fox's only enemies; eagles, too, carry them off, and even seals will kill them if they can. For their own part, Arctic foxes are primarily scavengers after wolves, polar bears, and human beings, often following such predators for many kilometers in hopes of snaring a bit of meat. In the short Arctic summer, they share with other foxes a taste for berries and other vegetation as well as for insects and rodents. Because of the harshness of his environment, the Arctic fox is accustomed to migrating southward in winter and northward in spring, maintaining contact with food supplies by so doing. Luckily, the Arctic fox's range does not coincide with

The two color phases of the Arctic fox, white for winter's snow (*left*) and "blue" for summer.

The raccoon dog, like the bat-eared fox, possesses distinctive facial markings that encourage ritual grooming. Although closely resembling a real raccoon, this foxlike animal has the long legs of a true canid.

---

that of agricultural man; if it did, the curiosity of these beautiful creatures would surely lead them to ruin.

The raccoon dog (*Nyctereutes procyonoides*, "Nocturnal Raccoonlike") is usually lumped with the foxes, if only by reason of size; although definitely a canid, the animal does not otherwise closely resemble any fox. About 75 centimeters long from nose to tip of tail, this weird animal really does look like a raccoon, even to the point of sporting a neat black mask across his face. He acts like one, too, preferring the banks of rivers and lakes in his native lands, which stretch from Japan through most of eastern China and much of Southeast Asia. Here he catches fish, crayfish and frogs, rodents and small birds, and shares the general foxy taste for berries and other fruits, especially acorns. Raccoon dogs further resemble raccoons in that they enter a period of winter dormancy in the colder parts of their range after having laid on a thick layer of fat in the autumn. Long hunted for their excellent flesh and thick fur, raccoon dogs have successfully been introduced to north-central Europe.

No discussion of the world's "foxes" could be complete without a look at the unique canids of South America. That continent has enjoyed an unusual history in that during the past 65,000,000 years it has for much of the time been isolated by an oceanic strait passing across what is now the Isthmus of Panama. Until about 4,000,000 or 5,000,000 years ago, South America had no advanced carnivorous fauna of the cat and dog variety that has long dominated the continents of Africa, Eurasia, and North America, which through geologic time have often been interconnected by land bridges; instead, the carnivores of South America were highly evolved marsupials related to the living American opossum but more closely resembling true dogs and cats because their econiches paralleled those of the northern placental carnivores. Once the land bridge to North America did return, the way was open for invasion by northern carnivores; these, being smarter and generally more efficient than the marsupials, quickly replaced them and experienced an adaptive radiation across that vast continent.

The most significant and widespread result of the canid invasion of South America was the evolution and diversification of a genus *Dusicyon*, including canids typical of that continent but paralleling in form and function most of the foxlike canids of the northern continents. Eight species of *Dusicyon*, all foxy both in appearance and in behavior, inhabit almost all of South America from the heights of the Andes (the Inca fox, *D. inca*), to the jungles of the Amazon basin (the various zorros, or Amazon foxes), to the high pampas of Chile and Argentina (the pampas fox, *D. griseus*). Largest of the genus is the culpeo fox (*D. culpaeus*), an inhabitant of the Andes, which at 1.5 meters in length is sometimes called the Andean wild dog. This species occasionally indulges in the unfoxlike behavior of hunting in packs, but such group activities are more the exception than the rule. One species of *Dusicyon*, the Falkland Islands dog (*D. australis*), became extinct in the nineteenth century after domestic dogs were introduced to its native habitat; it is thus the only canid so far, poor thing, to have been completely exterminated by human activity.

Yet another unique South American expression of canid evolution is the maned wolf (*Chrysocyon brachyurus*, "Golden Dog with a Broad Tail"), the "stilt fox" of the pampas, so called because of his long legs. The largest canid native to the continent, this animal is superbly adapted for the chase in open country, using his long legs to bound across the pampas after hares and other speedy herbivores. Unlike other large grassland canids, however, maned wolves do not hunt in packs.

In the rain forests of Amazonia lives the mysterious bush dog (*Speothos venaticus*, "Hunting Cave-wolf"—so called because his bones have been found in caves). Bush dogs are brown, short-legged animals of fox-size that inhabit jungles and thick brush near water. Excellent swimmers, they often leap into rivers when pursuing aquatic rodents or when being pursued themselves by human beings. They are social, living in groups of about fifteen adults centered around an alpha (dominant) male. Although widespread in range, they are rarely seen because of their nocturnal habits and inaccessible haunts. Still, many a bush dog cub has been taken into captivity, and on the whole these strange canids make gentle and affectionate pets. Alone among canids, bush dogs have but thirty-eight teeth, owing to a reduction in molar number from the usual 2/3 to 1/2. This is believed to be a reflection of their

The long-legged pampas maned wolf (*left*) and the low-slung nocturnal bush dog are unique South American canids.

almost entirely carnivorous diet, bush dogs having little use for grinding molars.

One tiny South American canid enjoys the ultracanid scientific name *Cerdocyon thous*, roughly translatable from the Greek as "Foxdog-wolf." This is the crab-eating fox of water's edge, found throughout the northeastern portion of the continent. The little crab-eaters, a third smaller than the common red fox, spend most of their time eating land crabs and other arthropods as well as scavenging in the manner of jackals; this cleansing activity, performed in the villages of the region, often endears the crab-eating fox to human beings, and many are tamed and kept as pets.

Last and rarest of our South American forms is the small-eared fox, or zorro (*Atelocynus microtus*, "Imperfect Dog with Tiny Ears"). Unusual among canids in that the female of the species is larger than the male, the small-eared fox is an inhabitant of the dense undergrowth of the Amazon basin.

The introduction to South America of red foxes has placed many of the native forms in jeopardy. Cleverer, more aggressive, and warier of man, Reynard overlaps most of these animals in econiche and is better at life in general. In fact, on a worldwide scale red foxes are probably faring better than any other wild predators; as we humans continue the killing of ever-greater numbers of wild animals, we may soon see a world in which the only significant wild predators remaining will be Reynard the Trickster and a few of his adaptable smaller canid relatives.

THE WILD HUNTING DOGS

So far, we have examined a branch of the canid family that specializes for the most part in the killing of smaller prey, the sort of hunting that requires only a swift snap and shake of the head in the kill. Such small prey is stealthy, and the foxes and other small canids that hunt it are also stealthy; they are, as we have seen, the most "catlike" of canids. When one sees a canid designed for such hunting, he thinks "fox." What, then, of the canids that we universally call "dogs"?

The entire makeup of the wild dogs as differentiated from "foxes" is reflective of their hunting habits; when we speak of a "wild dog," we generally mean a canid that seeks prey his own size or larger as a way of life. Such hunting is impossible for most predators, inasmuch as large prey is always well defended—it is strong, fleet, and often social in behavior. Here is where we begin to see the striking similarities between wild dogs and human beings, for the overcoming of large prey results in certain parallels between these two otherwise distantly related beings, convergences that ultimately resulted in the evolution of a new species: *Canis familiaris*, the domestic dog.

As we have seen, all mammals—indeed, all animal life—descend from small creatures. There are many advantages in small size, especially that of being able to maintain a large and diverse population on limited resources of food and space. It is no accident that insects are numerically by far the largest and most multiformed group of land animals; and among mammals, rodents exceed all the rest in number of individuals and species. In an ecologic context, "small is beautiful."

In essence, there is but one advantage in large size: the greater strength that comes with increasing bulk—a strength that, in herbivores, eliminates most predation by hunters their own size or smaller. Once dinosaurs disappeared from the scene, many groups of mammals therefore began experimenting with size increases, herbivorous forms beginning this tendency during the Paleocene. The natural variance in size among individuals in a world of little mammals, plus the easy availability of food and space in those days, permitted the bigger ones plenty of room in which to grow and reproduce, and so they did.

At first, the little predatory mammals were unable to mess with those first big herbivores by reason of the latters' strength alone. The big herbivores thus enjoyed a period during which they had a slow and easy life, one of perpetual eating, one free of strife. Reflecting this advantage is the corpulent and clumsy form implied by their fossil skeletons, for those early herbivores feared nothing in their world and consequently took nothing too seriously—especially exercise. The hiatus in predation was necessarily short-lived, however, for early predatory mammals enjoyed the same size variations as did their vegetarian relatives, and soon approached them in bigness.

By this time, the world was full of a silly-looking assemblage of experimental large mammals, all clumsy, all slow. The selective pressures exerted on herbivores by predators then took a new guise as size and strength alone no longer sufficed for protection. Aha! New herbivores appeared, faster ones—and predators followed suit. Now a world of fast, big predators and herbivores dominated the landscape. There is no stability, though, in the process of evolution. Changes in the herbivore brain began to appear, changes that permitted the social awareness necessary for a collective way of life. It takes a smart predator to invade a herd of aggressively defensive herbivores, and thus smarter predators—all descending from that old miacid line—began to appear.

Still, a mammalian ecosystem supports several times as many herbivores as it can the predators that feed on them. The comparatively few hunters affordable by an ecosystem, given the requirement that they maintain sufficient numbers to keep their gene-pool diversity intact, must by necessity be limited in individual size to permit sharing of resources. Thus, while some mammalian herbivores went on to elephant-size and larger, few terrestrial mammalian predators have ever been larger than, say, bears—and most are much smaller.

How, then, to exploit the big-predator econiche without growing too big oneself? The answer, of course, lies in social hunting, by which means a predator can, by sharing both work and booty with his family, overcome animals many times his own size. So advantageous, in fact, is social hunting of large prey that parallel social-hunting methods have arisen many times in vertebrate history. Each shares a complex of similar characteristics that span time and space to link the social hunters in an elite ecologic brotherhood. Most important of these characteristics is an ability to communicate with one another, for true social hunting implies the orderly sharing of the tasks of locating and killing prey, as well as built-in social restrains to ameliorate disputes between such lethally armed creatures before they swell into intraspecific murder.

The dinosaurs probably produced social hunters, likely candidates from the fossil record being the megalosaurs and dromaeosaurs, whose comparatively small size by no means limited them to small prey. Fast inhabitants of open lands, these terrible creatures left their birdlike tracks superimposed on the giant spoor of the great herbivorous sauropods they hunted; such huge prey no doubt required of predatory dinosaurs all of the sociability and elaborate ritual characteristic of mammalian social hunters.

In modern oceans, the killer whales of genus *Orcinus* are similarly sociable, linked by complex patterns of call and behavior as they overcome other whales many times their own size. Strikingly marked in black and white, killer whales can see one another well through the oceanic murk, in keeping with the requirement that social hunters maintain good visual contact.

On land, the Catlike Ones have also experimented with social hunting, most notably among the African spotted hyenas (*Crocuta crocuta*). Big beasts,

Megalosaurs appear to have been dinosaurian social hunters that killed prey far larger than themselves.

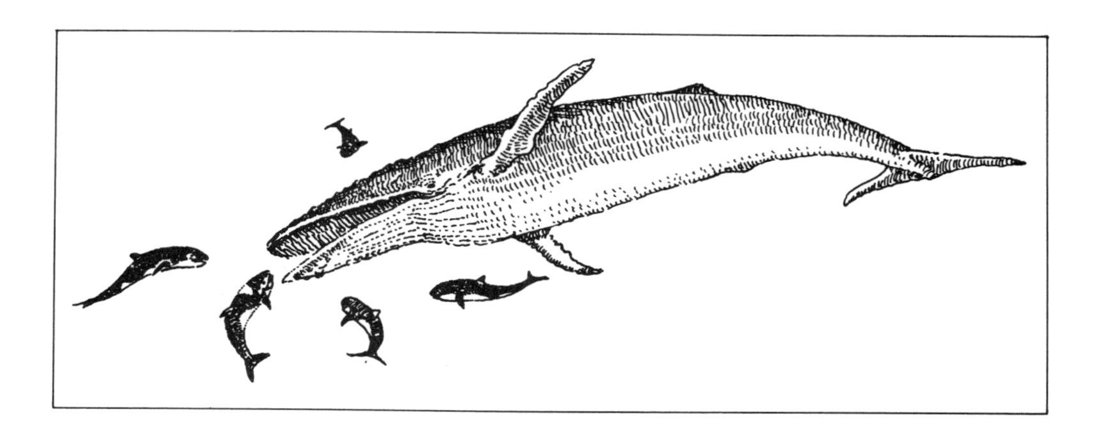

Modern social-hunting mammals include killer whales (*above*, shown attacking a baleen whale) and spotted hyenas (*below*, with wildebeeste).

superficially doglike in appearance but more closely related to mongooses and cats, spotted hyenas enjoy through their clannish sociability a success that extends their range across nearly all of sub-Saharan Africa. Formerly maligned in the public awareness as scavengers, hyenas are in some respects dominant among African predators, especially with regard to nighttime hunting. The African lions (as opposed to Asian lions) also hunt in groups, but these are mere aggregations—family prides—and lack the organization and communicative interaction typical of true social hunters. As a consequence, the group behavior of lions is marked by intranecine murder on a scale unequaled in tribes of true social hunters.

Of course, any discussion of social hunters would be positively anemic without mention of human beings; alone among primates, our kind entered this niche (comparatively late, as such things go) to compete with the hyenas and wild dogs of the world. Using tools and projectiles, human hunters once and for all circumvented the advantages conferred on herbivores by large size, in so doing producing the extinction of almost all of the world's giant mammals—but that is a story for later in the book.

There are three commonly recognized genera of the wild hunting dogs, each of which represents specializations to inhabiting different parts of the world rather than any fundamental differences in their social-hunting methods. All of them specialize in that unique canid tirelessness that we discussed earlier, relying on sheer endurance to overcome powerful prey that would be quite unavailable to creatures possessed of any less vitality. All wild dogs are superb runners and trotters, distance machines, able to press a herd for miles until some unhealthy individual falls out and can be captured. The long-distance canid trot, easy and graceful, can carry a wild dog for two days nonstop if need be, at a steady pace of up to 9 or 10 kilometers per hour (the stride of a healthy man at an easy trot or jog is about 7 km/hr). Breaking into a sprint, a fast wild dog can clear 45 km/hr for a couple of kilometers; a fast human being may make 23 km/hr for the same distance. Wild dogs have a speed advantage not only in their ancient adaptations for sprinting but also in their weight; the largest of them (the very, very few, most gigantic wolves) may weigh 60 kilograms, while an average adult man weighs about 70.

Being predators who seize their large prey with their mouths, the wild dogs sport long, stout jaws containing molars designed for the crushing of bones rather than for the grinding of vegetation as in the "foxes." The power of these jaws is enormous; a wild dog weighing 40 or so kilograms can easily maintain its grip on large prey even if lifted entirely off the ground and tossed about by its unlucky victim; measurements with specially designed bite scales suggest that the jaws of a large domestic dog can exert a pressure of some 300 kilograms (more than 600 pounds); those of wild dogs are probably even more powerful.

Most important to their way of life is the strong family orientation of wild dogs; in areas where they are undisturbed by human activity, they live in perennial packs, or tribes, comprising several generations. Connected with this sociability is the fact that all of them are food carriers; leaving nursing females and dependent young at their dens, the hunters set out for the kill and return laden with food—not only carried in the jaws but temporarily stored in the belly, to be regurgitated to the homebodies. The mobility of the hunt is in this way maximized even during the whelping seasons, ensuring everyone a share in the food supply of the tribe. Social mechanisms for sharing enable all, even the young and the weak, a place at table; pups and the elderly are amicably permitted to eat along with the prime hunters rather than being forced to wait for scraps as are, say, lion cubs.

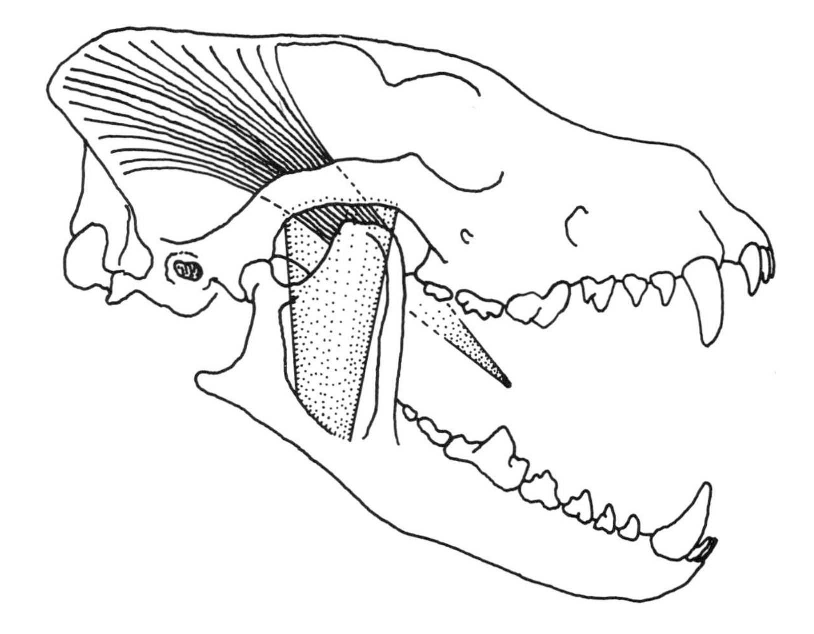

The skull of the Cape hunting dog, like that of all large wild canids, is a robust structure designed for the seizing of powerful prey. The temporal muscles (those whose fibers connect the crown of the lower jaw with the crest of the braincase) are so deployed that their force is strongest at the point of intersection between the carnassial teeth; the masseters, or chewing muscles (stippled), link the angle of the jaw with the broad cheekbone.

Another important aspect of the sociability of hunting dogs of all types is the fact that adults which have no pups of their own will "adopt" and raise youngsters whose mother has been incapacitated or killed. This is as true of males as it is of females; many litters of pups have been raised by "uncles" when the mothers have been lost. Coupled with this adoptive tendency is the general fascination for puppies held by adults. On returning from a hunt, the adults in all wild-dog species actively compete, stumbling over one another, to feed and play with the pups, and in general the relationship between young and adult in a pack is a delight to behold.

Perhaps most ancient of the wild-dog species is the Cape hunting dog, the sub-Saharan African representative of the wild-dog way of life. Outwardly, these are as doglike as dogs can be; specialized to coursing the vast savannas of Africa, Cape hunting dogs are given a separate generic status (*Lycaon*, which means, simply but inaccurately, "Wolf") because of their unique foot structure among the candids: they have four toes on both fore and hind feet, rather than the usual five toes on the forefoot and four behind. In addition, *Lycaon* has a real, honest-to-goodness functional collarbone—a rarity among canids, in most of whom this bone is but a cartilaginous remnant amid the

Cape hunting dogs are fond of family life; adults returning to the den from hunting regurgitate food to pups and play with them for hours at a time. Each dog is conspicuously mottled in black, brown, and white as an aid to individual recognition.

---

muscles of the shoulder. These characteristics evidence a long separate evolutionary history for *Lycaon*, a genus almost entirely restricted to Africa, although fragments of one member species have been found in a cave in Glamorganshire, Wales. This form, dubbed *L. anglicus*, seems to have moved north during the warm intervals between the vast Pleistocene glaciations when Europe was inhabited by elephants, hippopotamuses, monkeys, and other typically African mammals.

The Cape hunting dogs are often called "hyena dogs," and for a very good reason: like their more catlike namesakes, they are irregularly spotted (hence their specific name, *pictus*, "spotted")—and are, in fact, the only canids so marked. Because they are hunters in open lands and travel in groups, they appear to have evolved their odd coats in response to a requirement for individual recognition by sight over long distances; scientists who study the habits of Cape hunting dogs are easily able to follow the activities of individuals within a pack by observing the unique patterning of each dog's coat, and presumably the dogs work on the same information. Certainly, the spotting of Cape hunting dogs is not a camouflage, for these big black-brown-and-white animals are among the most strikingly conspicuous of predators in their native golden grasslands.

High visibility is, indeed, one of the hallmarks of the Cape hunting dog's style. They are primarily hunters by vision themselves, and their aggressive visibility also serves in their propensity for deliberately herding prey animals. The hunt is preceded by a little ritual during which the participants eagerly lick and nuzzle one another in what has been called an "arousal ceremony." Once all are properly excited, the dogs (in packs of up to fifty) approach their chosen herd of grazers, commonly antelope or zebra, and move along its perimeter in what has been described as a "slinking, horizontal walk" that is common to all wild dogs testing their prey. Often the dogs stand stock-still, watching the herd move by; presumably this period of observation enables them to identify an individual within the herd which is in some way behaviorally different from its fellows, for the success of a hunt is enhanced by the choice of a young, disabled, or otherwise unfit specimen.

If the above technique fails, the pack may approach the herd in a more aggressive manner, setting the grazers in motion, scattering them if possible, all the while observing their motion carefully though making no direct attacks. However the final selection is made, the pack really turns on the steam at last, sprinting after a suitable individual (sometimes several) and ignoring its fellows. The kill is usually made by disemboweling—like a frenzied group of sharks, the dogs, seizing their prey by any projecting part, cover it in a welter of wagging tails.

Within their societies, Cape hunting dogs have two distinct hierarchies, male and female, each with its own internal rules of behavior. Withal, however, they are friendly and orderly among themselves, especially with regard to the raising of young. Females bear their litters in the winter (May to July) of their subequatorial year, whelping as many as sixteen pups at a time in dens remodeled from the works of other burrowing mammals. Mothers remain in the dens with young pups and are fed by the rest of the pack after each hunt. The pups eat meat by the time they are a month old, and in a year may actively participate in the hunt as a new generation of pups is born and must be fed.

Cape hunting dogs and human beings have shared a long evolutionary history, for it was on the African savannas that human life as we know it first appeared. For some 3,000,000 years the small man-ape called *Australopithecus africanus* ("Southern Ape of Africa") and his kind perfected their own pack-hunting techniques among the grazers of Africa—often, perhaps, driving the hunting dogs from their rightful prey rather than killing their own. While the dogs are wisely afraid of modern humanity, it is not difficult to

Australopithecines, while comparatively small-brained and barely a meter and a half tall, were excellent runners and seem to have hunted in groups, killing such formidable prey as baboons with bones and other clublike weapons. From animals very like the australopithecines is descended all of humanity.

imagine these efficient carnivores attacking an occasional lone man-ape and hauling him off in those long-gone times before humans were really human (the man-apes, while fully bipedal, stood only four or so feet tall, and must have been comparatively easy prey before they evolved their own advanced hunting societies). Even today, many people are afraid of hunting dogs and their nocturnal pack-hunting ecological counterparts, the hyenas; perhaps this discomfort is a remnant of the distant times when the dogs, with the big cats, were the most dangerous predators on our own kind.

Still, hunting dogs tame well if caught as young pups, and there exist records suggesting that the ancient Egyptians used them in the coursing of antelope. Otherwise, however, there is no evidence that human beings and Cape hunting dogs have interacted much, except as ecological competitors. Today, the dogs are often implicated in the killing of domestic livestock and are in some places relentlessly persecuted by farmers. Nonetheless, *L. pictus* enjoys one of the largest ranges among the social carnivores, in places even extending its territory as the more solitary African predators—big cats—die off at the hands of man.

Rather closer to domestic dogs in appearance are the dholes, or red dogs (*Cuon alpinus*, "Mountain Dog"), of the Indian subcontinent and Southeast Asia. Representing a wild-dog invasion of forest habitats, dholes are much feared by the human beings whose ranges they share, and are said to attack even tigers, so efficient are they as hunters. Like all wild dogs, dholes raise their young at home bases from which they range over many square kilometers, killing wild pigs, deer, rodents, and other herbivores, and, occasionally, small carnivores such as foxes. In addition, dholes are fond of the comparatively defenseless domesticated herbivores; thus, like other wild carnivores, they are suffering at the hands of stockmen as agriculture uses up ever more land.

Like Cape Hunting dogs, dholes represent a comparatively ancient separation from the main branch of the canid family tree. Unlike other canids, they lack the last lower molars, a specialization related to their nearly entirely carnivorous diet; in consequence, their muzzles are short and stout, giving their faces a rounded appearance. As do most canids, dholes display considerable variation in color: the typical specimen is fox-red with a black-tipped tail and light undersides, but within a single litter some individuals may be almost black, others tawny-yellow, and some nearly white. Indeed, with their many colors and marking patterns, groups of dholes are sometimes mistaken for domestic dogs even by experienced observers.

Inhabiting as they do areas that are still comparatively sparsely populated by human beings, dholes and Cape hunting dogs represent remnants of a prehuman order of carnivores whose activities are as yet largely unchanged by human activity. We can envision these spectacular animals disappearing as the remaining untouched areas of their ranges come under increased cultiva-

The short-haired dhole of India and Southeast Asia resembles some domestic dogs in size and coloring.

tion, and the time left to them as wild hunters is probably short. One hopes that more observers will choose to live among them for a time to learn their ways and share them with the rest of us before their ancient societies become unrecognizable fragments of the old hunting ways.

GENUS *CANIS*

Here are the "real" dogs at last, the worldwide genus of higher social canids from which springs our own domesticated version in all its myriad forms. Genus *Canis* ("Dog") is in some ways a puzzle, even though it is one of the most intensively studied and best known of animal groups and therefore enjoys almost as many separate classifications as there are taxonomists to classify it.

Part of the problem of classification lies in the genus's essentially monotypical—homogenized—physical structure. In the classification followed in this book, *Canis* represents nine species distributed over all of the world's continents, including Antarctica, and most islands to boot. This immense distribution is, of course, based in part on the activities of human beings; after all, one of the species is *C. familiaris*, which lives wherever human beings live. Within *Canis* all nine species can and do interbreed to produce fertile offspring, although this particular criterion of classification—successful interbreeding—has traditionally served to define single species rather than genera.

The problem with *Canis* is exemplified by the evolution and distribution of the coyote, or "prairie wolf" (*C. latrans*, "barking dog"), of North America. Coyotes are canids originally specialized to ecosystems incapable of supporting larger predators—such habitats as deserts and desert edges and the alpine regions of mountain ranges. Here the coyote pursued its cheerful canid lifestyle until the coming of the Europeans, who wrought within a couple of human generations such vast ecological changes on the North American landscape that none of it can be said to remain untouched by human hands.

Pioneers crossing the prairies and arid regions of the American West were perfectly justified in dubbing coyotes "prairie wolves," for these little dogs are in fact small wolves; where the ranges of wolf and coyote (from *coyotl*, the Nahuatl name for the animal) overlap, the canid inhabitants of the region usually exhibit every degree of shading and size from the little (up to 20 kilograms) coyote to the large (up to 60 kilograms) wolf typical of circumpolar regions throughout the Northern Hemisphere. One canine species, the red wolf (*C. niger*—which means, oddly, "black dog"), of the southeastern United States, appears to be a sort of wolf-coyote cross, but this is a species soon doomed to extinction, with perhaps fewer than a hundred individuals remaining. In all, coyotes may be regarded as comprising a specialized midget race within the larger family of their lupine cousins.

Another facet of the canid classification problem is apparent in the wake of the disruption wrought by the European invasion of North America. Like most humans, the pioneers did not coexist peacefully with true wolves, and within two centuries nearly all the wolves of the continental forty-eight American states were extinct as a result of human depredations. The coyote, however, is a dog specialized to difficulty and to regions of meager resources, and is also smaller and less visible both physically and ecologically than its larger relatives. Thus man has been unable (although, God knows, he tries!) to extirpate the coyote, as he did the larger and more ecologically delicate wolf, whose former successes were dependent on social stability and the constant availability of large populations of big-game prey.

The extermination of the wolf opened an econiche throughout its former pan–North American range, an econiche for canid predators. It was an impoverished econiche, true, in that with the wolf went most of its traditional prey, the bison and other large herbivores native to the region. Like most modern human beings, Europeans (especially!) tend to arrogate to themselves most of the biomass of the regions they inhabit, and thus North American animal biomass has been converted into domestic animals and human beings in unprecedented numbers. And what North American member of genus *Canis* is most suited to impoverished ecosystems? The coyote.

Once the wolf was driven out, coyotes found open to them vast new ranges free of canid competition. Originally a Western beast, the coyote was quick to capitalize on the situation, extending its range eastward to the Mississippi and beyond. Here, invading the woodlands of the Midwest and Atlantic states, the little wolf has prospered, and here several new subspecies have evolved.

Coyotes moving into eastern Canada appear to have interbred successfully with the relict local populations of timber wolves, producing large coyotes (or small wolves—who's to say?) with thicker coats that are well suited to the cold, wet climates of the East. The new breed is successfully invading New Hampshire and Maine, and is apparently very much at home in these

The coyote, whose scientific name means "barking dog," is actually a melodious songster who rarely barks.

---

former habitats of the true wolves. But what kind of animal *is* this? Is it a "wolf"? Or is it a "coyote"? The problem is further compounded by the fact that such wild canids can also interbreed easily with domestic dogs, so that there is probably some admixture of the latters' genes in the new Eastern canid.

Such stories abound wherever human beings disrupt the habitats of canids. In Asia Minor, the various jackal "species" display smooth gradations in form between one another and domestic dogs wherever their ranges overlap to permit interbreeding, and are said in some mountainous areas to be nearly indistinguishable from the remaining wolves. In areas where the ranges of wolves and domestic dogs overlap, in fact, interbreeding among them is sometimes artificially encouraged. Thus this taxonomic teapot-tempest is further complicated by the admixture of the domestic form.

Consider, for example, the Great Dane and the dachshund; presented to an honest taxonomist who had never before seen a domestic dog, each would instantly be recognized as a carnivore—perhaps even as a member of family Canidae. Beyond this, however, they would probably be classed not only in different species but probably in different genera as well. Not only will these two forms not interbreed (without mechanical intervention, such as artificial insemination), but they are so different with regard to almost every criterion available to our hypothetical taxonomist that there is no way in heaven or on earth that these two might slip into the same species in an honest anatomical classification. The same person, however, would probably place wolves, coyotes, jackals, and some forms of domestic dogs, such as dingoes, large shepherd dogs, and huskies, within the same species if these were considered from a strictly anatomical viewpoint.

The Great Dane dog and wirehaired dachshund bitch shown here, although classed within the same species, *Canis familiaris*, could not mate, because of obvious technical difficulties.

An impartial taxonomist might actually assign to the true dogs a specific status, perhaps "*Canis canis*," regarding them as a single polytypic species much as we do the many variants of human beings around the world. Thus the different canine types—wolves, domestic dogs, coyotes, and so on—might be listed as races: *Canis canis lupus, C. c. familiaris, C. c. latrans*. But this has not yet been done, at least officially, so we must conform in this book to the puzzling classifications of traditional taxonomy.

Taxonomy aside, we find in members of genus *Canis* the logical endpoint of canid evolution as seen in the ecosystems surrounding the North Pole. These are the social hunters (plus some secondarily generalized hunter-scavengers) that dominated the social-predator econiches of the cooler parts of the world when human beings first invaded those areas less than a million years ago, and they remain the most successful large wild predators left to the Northern Hemisphere.

Perhaps the most important aspect of genus *Canis* separating it from other canids (such as foxes) that share its range is its extreme sociability; only in severely disrupted ecosystems like that of North America, and only in a few species (coyotes, for example), do groups as small as nuclear families exist among members of the genus, and such small families are always indicative of ecologic disruption. Undisturbed, most members of the genus form lifetime associations and pick lifetime-preferred mates—among old societies of wolves, the killing of one of a "married" pair may result in the death (of a broken heart?) of the other. Such sociability, with its inborn potential for learning rules and traditions, is the primary factor resulting in the domestication of dogs, with their adaptability for functioning within the highly organized societies of human beings.

Viewed diagrammatically and as a single aggregation, *Canis* seems to be centered in range on the North Pole in the form of the wolf (*C. lupus*, "Wolf-dog"). The other wild species are smaller versions of the wolf, each inhabiting the edges of the old lupine range and each adapted to some degree for eking out a living in semiarid situations in which much scavenging and secretiveness are *de rigueur* as a way of coping with conditions of attenuated biomass. In comparatively recent times (within the last million years) some of these smaller wild dogs have penetrated sub-Saharan regions, where they coexist with larger predators by specializing primarily in scavenging rather than by competing with established forms. These "interlopers" include, for example, the southern African black-backed jackal (*C. mesomelas*) and the side-striped jackal (*C. adustus*), plains dwellers whose mode of life is one of snatching food from the kills of hyenas, Cape hunting dogs, and big cats—although, under the right circumstances, these little dogs will hunt in packs on

The black-backed (*left*) and side-striped jackals are African social rodent-hunters and scavengers.

their own, killing such prey as small antelope much in the manner of the true wolves of the north.

One jackal may have evolved as a direct result of early human interference with ecosystems: the golden jackal (*C. aureus*) inhabits precisely the range of greatest concentration of human fossils. Here, in North Africa and southern Asia, human beings early killed off many of the larger herbivores on which ancestral wolves preyed, and domesticated most of the rest. In so doing, like later men everywhere, they attenuated the local ecosystems to such a point that deserts and semideserts swiftly appeared, biomass becoming ever rarer and concentrated for the most part around areas of intensive human activity—for humans always seem to gather biomass to themselves. In such areas the scavenging golden jackal is very successful in the manner of the American coyote (which physically resembles the golden jackal in almost every respect as a result of convergent evolution between these two widely separated forms).

Within the ancient man-made ecosystems of Asia Minor and North Africa, the golden jackal has found an enduring place as scavenger, occasional competitor, sharer of disease (most notably rabies), and even mythological character. One of the most conspicuous gods of the ancient Egyptian pantheon was the jackal Anubis, conductor of the souls of the dead. A personification of the man-made econiche of the jackal, Anubis is the cleansing god, the guardian of the gates of the underworld and a reflection of the well-known fondness of jackals for the dead, human as well as animal. Like the coyote, the jackal is

The lightly built golden jackal, a wild canid associated with agricultural civilizations of North Africa and the Near East since ancient times.

---

doing very well in a world overpopulated by human beings, his numbers remaining stable or even increasing throughout his vast range. Almost indistinguishable from the golden jackal, and very likely a subspecies, is the Ethiopian form *C. simensis* ("Simenian dog"), yet another monkey wrench in the works of canine classification.

As we have seen, the real wolf (*C. lupus*), seems to lie at the center of its genus in both distribution and evolutionary progress. The wolf is the quintessential wild dog, the largest and most spectacular of canids and the most efficient predator (besides humankind) of the circumpolar regions of Eurasia and North America. In the standard reference work on the species, Dr. L. David Mech's *The Wolf*, are listed some thirty-two races of wolves inhabiting all of Europe, Asia, and North America south to central Mexico. Of these, most are now extinct or threatened with extermination at the hands of man, the foremost predator, who brooks no competition. Still, where undisturbed, wolves are the only remaining significant wild predators of such larger herbivores as deer and the many types of wild oxen; indeed, wolves and these herbivores are so intimately intertwined evolutionarily that they are essentially creations of one another—the wolf mirrors the deer (or elk, or reindeer, or bison), and the deer mirrors the wolf, as noted before.

Like human beings, wolves are products of the Pleistocene, that recent epoch of upheaval (as it is often called in paleontology texts) during which, for some 3,000,000 years, the climate switched from warm to cold and back again in a dizzying progression of glaciations. Like humans also, wolves are

Most capable of social hunters, human beings invaded the world's northlands in search of such giant prey as the imperial mammoth shown here. Wolves (*left*) probably early took to following such men and scavenging from their kills.

superb adapters, and they capitalized on their social habits and ability to learn as they coped with the insane and terrible climatic changes of the epoch. Having originated as hunters of the larger herbivores, wolves in groups are capable of overcoming any modern northern herbivore up to and including the formidable wild oxen such as musk-oxen and bison (although, being sensible animals, they prefer tackling meeker creatures such as deer, the killing of which involves less danger to the hunter).

About 100,000 years ago, human beings first invaded the northern regions of Eurasia in a big way, hunting the largest of herbivores, primarily those inaccessible to wolves by reason of immense size and strength. In those days, the north was inhabited by a variety of elephants, rhinoceroses, and other creatures whose sheer mass and might permitted them to graze unconcerned among such formidable predators as the wolves and great cats that shared their inhospitable habitats at the edges of the Pleistocene ice fields. It remained for a carnivorous creature who could circumvent such vast strength to invade the giant-herbivore–hunter econiche, and man was the one to do so.

Utilizing projectiles, fire, and traps, primitive humans easily overcame such giants as mammoths and rhinoceroses, slow beasts at best; thus, in the beginning, humans and wolves probably shared the tundra forests of Eurasia amicably enough, their econiches rarely overlapping enough for direct competition between them to take place. Fleeter and with more endurance in the chase than their human counterparts, wolves concentrated their diet on deer and the like (as they now do), while human beings preyed intensively on the easily captured giants.

Giants, however, are never particularly large in numbers. Because the feeding of one giant of whatever species requires vast quantities of forage, an ecosystem by necessity supports fewer of them than it does smaller herbivores, this being particularly noticeable in cold regions where vegetation grows slowly in sharply seasonal patterns. Thus the human invasion of the north marked the rapid decline of the giants, so that the advance of man coincides precisely with the rapid extinction of the northern giants throughout the world. Between 50,000 and 10,000 years ago, perhaps 80 percent of the genera of mammals weighing more than 100 kilograms became extinct, including both the giant herbivores and the specialized predators (certain great cats, for instance) that had theretofore lived off them in an ecologically balanced manner. The large-mammal fauna remaining in cool parts of the world in the last few thousand years largely comprises those mammals which by means of speed, secretiveness, or sheer aggressiveness were able to circumvent the wiles of Stone Age hunters.

Now, it happens that just such mammals are the preferred prey of wolves, so that we mark a period between about 30,000 and 10,000 years ago during which human beings were forced by their own excesses to begin competing with wolves. We are still seeing this competition throughout both Eurasia and North America as our kind, improving the efficiency of its deadly hunting methods, mops up the last of the great wild herds of game. This contest between wolf and human, in which the sounds of modern firearms are underscoring the last sorry chapters, has resulted in one of the most intimate symbioses of disparate species known to us, a relationship strikingly reflected in our history, folklore, and biology.

With that competition in mind, it is instructive to examine the folkloric aspects of our relationships with wolves, and by so doing to gain a fuller picture of the thousands of years during which man and wolf have interacted and of how our two modes of hunting came at last to interfere with each other. As is natural in a rivalry between species, each became of great importance to the other; nowhere is this importance better reflected than in the spoken traditions of humankind. Certainly the similarities between the societies of men and those of wolves were obvious to our ancestors. The "speech" of wolves, carrying across the lonely forests and tundras of the Pleistocene, was from the beginning a background music for the fur-clad human hunters,

While occurring in a variety of colors (even within the same family, as suggested here) and races, wolves are all characterized by a mobility and readability of expression that is a delight to behold.

---

and clans of lupine hunters were always visible. Among the few remaining northern hunters of today, such as Eskimos, Siberians, and American Indians, the wolf is thus personalized as a sort of four-legged human being; indeed, many of these consummate human hunters claim to be able to understand the song of wolves, to be able to determine by means of these eerie hoots and howls the location of prey and the movement of distant groups of men.

Such understanding is reflective of ecosystems in which, there being food enough for all, wolves and human beings coexist comparatively amicably. Once the human beings of Asia Minor began domesticating wild herbivores in response to diminishing supplies of wild game, however, the situation rapidly changed. Here, competition between the two species intensified to an actually adversary relationship, and here the folklore of wolves was born. One need only consider the tales of Little Red Ridinghood, the Boy Who Cried "Wolf!", and other such universal and horrific children's stories to see the direction in which agricultural society has taken our relationship with *Canis lupus.*

Surely, as human beings penetrated farther and farther into the north, they occasionally fell prey to wolves. In the days before firearms, a lone man would have been virtually defenseless against a pack, but isolated individuals must have survived to tell of the ruin wrought by man-eaters. Early on, however, selective pressures by human beings—the killing, that is, of over-confident wolves—seems to have evolved in the animals a universal fear of man. After all, a wolf has no defense but running speed against such a danger as a group of malevolent human beings, and the pressure against man-eaters was no doubt relentless. Rarely will a healthy wild wolf approach a healthy human very closely nowadays, and interaction between the two species nearly always results in the flight of the wolf. Still, wolves and men do interact, and the tale of the progress of this interaction is a fascinating one.

From the beginning, of course, humans recognized wolves as superb hunters; being themselves hunters, men admired their canine counterparts and sought to adopt some of their prowess through magic, such as the magic of names. Thus, for instance, the naming of Norsemen after wolves—Beowulf ("War Wolf") being perhaps the most famous example. Moreover, the Norsemen called their warships "seawolves," and, in assigning the wolf as companion to Odin, chief of their gods, capped their admiration with Asgardian honor.

Similarly, the ancient Celts envisioned their horned nature god Cernunnos as being accompanied by a wolf or two on his travels. There is, of course, an underside to man's relationship with wolves. The Norsemen equipped their underworld with Fenris-wolf, who was bound with a magic chain by the god Tyr (who lost his sword hand in so doing). This wolf-being symbolized chaos and the everlasting ice fields that would one day return to engulf the world; he was perhaps a remnant of some racial memory of the glaciers that once covered much of Europe, and of the wolves that shared with our ancestors the hunting along the edge of the groaning ice.

Similarities in social organization and habits between humans and wolves also resulted in the complex of myths that may be dubbed lycanthropy (from the Greek words meaning "wolf" and "man"). Stories of children raised by wolves, for instance, abound in areas where the ranges of the two species overlap; Rome is said to have been founded by two such youngsters, Romulus and Remus. Lycanthropy is even more closely associated with wolf-cult behavior, in which people adopted the wolf as their totem and sought to emulate its behavior. It has been suggested, for instance, that Romulus and Remus were raised by wolf-cult foster parents.

No account of lycanthropy could be complete without mention of werewolves (from ancient Teutonic words meaning "man-wolf"). During medieval times, werewolves seem to have troubled many European settlements, and legends of werewolf hangings are quite common. In such cases, the criminal is said to have reverted to his canid form in death. It is possible, then, that the wolf cults survived for some time the gradual Christianization of Europe, troubling for many centuries the propagandists of the Church.

As we have seen, at one time wolves shared nearly the entire northern world with human beings. Europe was so well populated by the big dogs that our documentation of their gradual extirpation reads like a chronicle: wolves were eliminated from England during the late fifteenth and early sixteenth centuries, during the reign of Henry VII; they disappeared from Scotland during the eighteenth century, but according to legend they may have lingered there as late as 1848; they were gone from Ireland by 1821.

In Western Europe, a few remaining enclaves of wolves may survive in mountainous regions—the Alps, Pyrenees, and the like—and some still inhabit the Italian peninsula, where they become more visible during hard winters. In Eastern Europe, wolves are more common; from Greece to Hungary, the animals are still breeding despite efforts by stockmen to have them eliminated. The closely monitored Scandinavian wolves, however, are doomed, numbering perhaps fifty in all—a sorry state of affairs in the old lands of Odin!

In Asia, wolves seem to inhabit much of their old range throughout the present-day Soviet Union and China, although their numbers there are severely reduced. The last Japanese wolf was reported in 1904. In North America, relict populations survive on Isle Royale, in Lake Superior, insulated from "sport" hunting by water and the National Park System; in Superior National Forest of northern Minnesota; perhaps in Michigan's Upper Peninsula; and, just possibly, in some isolated parts of the Rocky Mountains. Unfortunately, probably fewer than two hundred of these magnificent animals survive in the continental United States, and Mexico's remaining mountain population is equally threatened. Northern Canada and Alaska probably still support some fifty thousand wolves, but affluent and strident "sport" hunters, with their airplanes, snowmobiles, and telescope-equipped rifles, will likely soon exterminate them as well.

Wolves are not hunted for food; nor, in North America at least, are they hunted any longer for the protection of domestic animals. No, they are now hunted for "fun," by men who, unsure of the testosterone levels in their own blood, must "prove" themselves by slaying our remaining wolves with weapons better suited to warfare between human beings. Still eager to suggest that wolves are "detrimental to wild game," such men ignore the fact that at the time of the European invasion of North America, there was incomparably more wild game—and wolves, too—than remains for our appreciation today. In the biomass-collection game, human beings are supreme, and other animals, including wolves, fall by the wayside.

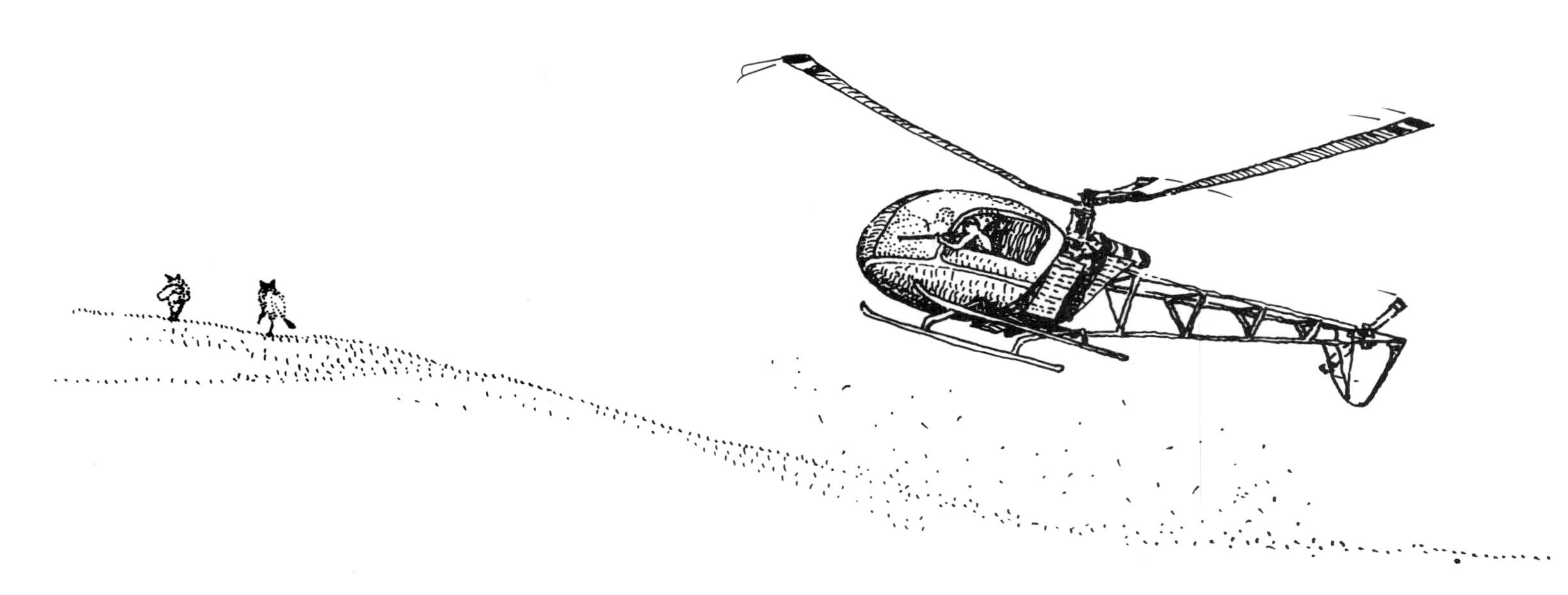

The disparity between modern wolf-hunting "sportsmen" and their prey might seem almost ludicrous, were it not for the fact that the wolves must die to prop the faltering egos of their murderers.

With modern advances in ethology—the study of the behavior of animals in the wild—we are coming to realize again what was known by our hunting ancestors: wolves, too, are "people," social beings with family groups close-knit by tradition and, yes, love. As our understanding of *Canis lupus* improves, we begin to see our relationship with the species as one of unilateral genocide and the potential of irremediable loss to ourselves with the extinction of our wild cousins. Contemporary ethologists and other biologists are producing volumes on the life and ways of wolves—superb volumes all, some of which are listed at the end of this book. With the wide availability of such works, perhaps enough of us will become acquainted with the elegant wolf mind that a public outcry will finally bury the efforts of "sportsmen" to destroy these splendid beasts. But the extinction of wolves approaches quickly, and much needs doing. Whether or not the wolves survive will be a true measure of the wisdom and humanity of human beings. The extinction of the wolves, if it does come about, will probably presage our own, and not by many years.

DOMESTICATION

At some point, then, human beings and wolves came to occupy the same econiche, as hunters of big game throughout the Northern Hemisphere. As competition between the two species intensified, societies of wolves began to give way to societies of human beings, so that we now inhabit a world of some five thousand *million* human beings and perhaps a hundred thousand wolves. Once probably about equal in numbers, human beings and wolves both now stare into the empty eye sockets of the Fourth Horseman, Extinction—too few wolves, too many people. Wolves will not die without leaving progeny, however. We and they have shared too many spaces, too many hard times, and, ever adaptable in the true canid manner, wolves early abandoned many of their old ways in an easy transition to the new, man-dominated world.

One might say in retrospect that the two northern social hunters, man and wolf, "interbred" on a social level to create a new species. Certainly, from their earliest meeting they were closely associated both spatially and ecologically, and both were changed by the association. The result, of course, is the domestic dog (*Canis familiaris*) in all of its strange and wonderful forms. Of all Canidae, the domestic form enjoys the widest range and the greatest numbers, for *C. familiaris* and human beings mill about the earth from pole to pole in vast and daily increasing numbers. In America alone, perhaps as many as eighty million dogs, about one for every three people, share the food supplies of the nation.

The gradation between wild and domesticated canids is so smooth as occasionally to defy analysis. Certainly one may easily distinguish a wolf from, say, a pointer dog. But what of the husky, the malamute, and the Arctic wolves? A group of such canids (and they do associate—are encouraged, in

One of the few characteristics sharply distinguishing a husky dog from a wolf is the "sickle tail" of the former; wolves and huskies are still crossed to maintain sledge-dog vitality.

fact, to do so by human beings) presents a uniformly wolfish aspect indeed. And what of the occasional wolf, raised from infancy by human beings, wagging his tail and playing with a human being? Is he a "domesticated wolf" or a "wild dog"? Or both? Or neither?

There are, of course, physical characteristics that serve to distinguish most domestic dogs from their wild relatives, and these traits are discernible both in living animals and in their skeletal remains. Among the living, we remark the enormous variation among domestic dogs in size alone—from 2 kilograms in Chihuahuas and other toy breeds to 100 kilograms in some mastiffs. Moreover, most domestic dogs exhibit a broad set of characteristics that may be subsumed under the term neoteny (the retention in adults of infantile or even embryonic characteristics). As an example, most domestic dogs share to some extent in a "lop-ear" conformation in which the ears hang limply at the sides of the head, but all wild canids sport erect, mobile ears from shortly after birth onward. Even in such straight-eared breeds as German shepherd dogs, the stiffening of the ears occurs far later in puppyhood than it does among wild canids. In this connection it is interesting to observe that the husky or malamute puppy's ears stand erect a good deal sooner than do those of the shepherd type, albeit still later than those of wolf pups.

Also neotenous is the "sickle tail" of domestic dogs. In wild canids, the tail is normally straight and carried at a downward-pointing angle when not in use as a social semaphore. In wild pups, however, the tail is a silly spike carried upward-pointing in a manner engaging to their parents and human observers alike. The tails of almost all domestic adult dogs curve upward even when they are at rest, and the universality of this trait is a sure indicator that neoteny was selected for at an early date in the process of domestication.

Some domestic races even have helical tails; such breeds as bulldogs and pugs, with their ridiculous twisted knots by way of tails, carry the characteristic to its extreme.

Yet another neotenous trait in domestic dogs is the bark. Adult wild canids bark only when defending their dens, in order to draw attention to themselves and lead predators away. Their pups, however, bark all the time, and so do most adult domestic dogs. The skulls of domestic dogs also show certain infantile aspects. Generally speaking, such skulls laid on a table will rest on their carnassial teeth and the rear of the skull, while the skull of a wolf rests on its canine teeth and the base of the skull. Of course, domestic dogs do not, as a rule, survive by pulling down large prey, as do their wolfish cousins, and so their jaws are generally shorter in proportion to skull length than are those of wolves. This particular neotenous characteristic may have originated as an environmental rather than a genetic trait of dogs, for tame wolves also show shorter jaws than do their wild parents, probably because they are fed commercial dog food rather than being forced to exercise their jaws constantly in the killing of big prey. Still, the short jaws of domestic dogs produce a "stop," or forehead bulge, which is infantile in character; early domesticators of dogs appear to have selected for this intelligent-puppy look from the beginning.

All wild dogs have erect ears as adults, but many domestic dogs retain infantile "lop-ears" throughout their lives.

Interestingly, the decrease in jaw length offers us a look at conditions that may have preceded the domestication of dogs. Archaeological evidence shows clearly that Stone Age human beings were much given to killing entire herds of herbivores, stampeding them with fire and projectiles until the animals became mired in swamps or threw themselves over cliffs. For the wolves with whom these men shared their habitat, such wasteful hunting must have pre-

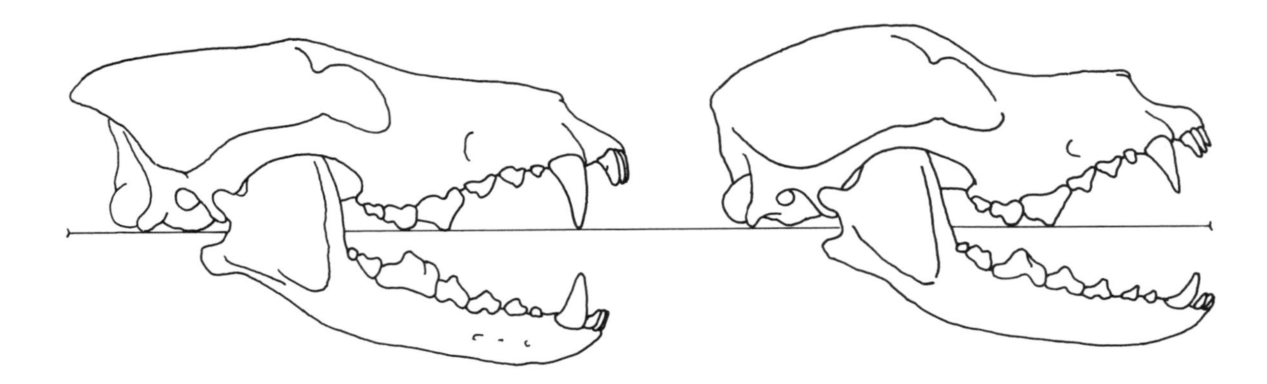

The skull of a wolf (*left*) placed on a flat surface usually rests on its canines and the base of the skull; that of a typical domestic dog rocks on its carnassial teeth because of the shortening of the jaws accompanying the process of domestication.

sented unprecedented opportunities for gorging; we can see from the many mass-kill sites that only a few of the dead herbivores were actually butchered by their human killers, the rest being left to rot in a manner sharply contradicting the modern myths that propose that Stone Age hunters were somehow so totally in tune with their environments that they wasted nothing. Because wolves are fleeter than humans, it is probable that they themselves rarely suffered depredation at the hands of early man; it is equally probable that bands of wolves took to following the wasteful human hunters, cleaning up after them and gradually abandoning their own dangerous hunting methods for the safer expedient of scavenging human kills. Knowing that tamed wolves grow shorter jaws than do their wild parents, we can easily envision entire tribes of wolves whose easy man-following ways essentially crippled them when it came to real wolfish hunting, so that over periods of thousands of years such tribes became at least partly dependent on their unwitting human benefactors.

With the gradual extinction of the giant herbivores of the north, the wolf-human symbiosis took a new turn. Human hunters came to specialize to a greater degree in the hunting of herding herbivores such as reindeer, wild cattle, and wild sheep, animals on which wolves had already preyed for millennia. As we have noted, social canids are able to assess herds for weak specimens and to "cut" these from the group; no doubt the wolves following human beings shared this "cutting" ability, which was obviously of use to their human cohorts. From their camp-following scavenger niche, then, dogs graduated to one of active participation in the hunt, and in so doing for the first time gained real recognition for their usefulness. Thus, during the period archaeologists call the Mesolithic, which extended from about 20,000 to 10,000 years ago, a time of transition in which prey was mainly of the herding type, hunters appear to have selected good herders from among the wolves following them.

This was no great leap of the imagination; wolf pups are born to participate in organized social groups, and human beings live in just such units. Captured wolf pups undergo a period of socialization between their third week, when they first emerge from the den, and about their third month of age. During this "imprinting" period, they meet the rest of the pack and learn its internal order of dominance, and during this time they form their lifelong attachments—they learn whom to love. Wolf pups raised by human beings easily transfer their affections to their foster parents, growing into the human "pack"—but only if they are captured during or before the critical period of socialization.

There is a crucial difference, however, between a tame, well-socialized wolf and a dog: the wolf learns to love human beings much as he would have loved wolves. Thus, for instance, he will persist in greeting his human friends with the affectionate ritual muzzle-bite that in wolves is an invitation to play. But this biting is not appreciated by most human beings—a 50-kilogram wolf standing on his hind legs to give one a snap to the nose while resting his forepaws on one's shoulders is troublesome, to say the least. The dog, on the other hand, has undergone millennia of selection for an understanding that human beings *are not dogs* and are not to be treated as such. In this context, it is notable that certain huskies and the like retain the affectionate muzzle-bite and in other respects treat their human symbionts as equals rather than as masters, and so these noble beasts are suitable only for strong-willed people. My Rufus, too, insists on treating us all as he might a coyote family, and we have never been able to train him away from that loving muzzle-bite.

Although often given separate-species status, the Australian dingo is probably a formerly domesticated dog returned to the wild.

The earliest clearly domesticated dogs—those showing skeletal features visibly divergent from those of plain wolves—are found in camp deposits from Australia that have been carbon-dated to 30,000 B.P. (before the present). These are clearly dogs of the type now known as dingoes and ordinarily classified as a separate canid species (*C. dingo*)—although for our purposes it is more suitable that they be regarded as a domesticated race in a feral (returned to the wild) state. Dingoes were carried to Australia by the ancestors of the aborigines thousands of years ago, when glaciers still held much of the world's water frozen at the poles. This resulted in lowered sea levels worldwide, permitting early men in fragile canoes to cross the narrows between the Asiatic mainland and Australia. Descended from domesticated dogs of a sort closely related to the southern Asian wolf, early dingoes found themselves in a canid paradise when introduced to Australia, where no native placental carnivores had ever existed. Occupying the "canid" econiche instead were the thylacines, or marsupial "wolves," creatures which did not hunt socially but which paralleled in many ways the true canids, most especially in their ability to run tirelessly and bring down large prey such as kangaroos. Unfortunately for the thylacine, dingoes are very like wolves in both intelligence and social organization, and within a very few thousand years they had spread across Australia and displaced the thylacines, which are now extinct in all but a few remote areas of Tasmania.

Despite its long history as a feral carnivore in Australia and nearby islands, the dingo was easily recognized by the first European invaders as a sort of domestic dog. With its short, tawny coat, white undersides, and rounded, erect ears, the animal looks much like any mutt and breeds readily with domestic dogs. Dingoes are occasionally tamed by modern aborigines, who, however, make no effort to breed them. Presumably, the dingoes that crossed the waters with their human benefactors were similar in habits to those wolves that early men found useful in hunting; indeed, the dingo is closest skeletally to the small southeastern Asian wolf *Canis lupus pallipes* ("white-footed wolf"). Wild dingoes eat sheep on their nocturnal hunting forays, and so are hunted in turn by stockmen, who have extirpated them from much of Australia. On the other hand, they are well adapted to the island continent's semiarid interior and are often bred with European sheepdogs to produce superior herd captains.

Because the dingo is a unique placental carnivore in pre-European Australia, its remains are easily identified, and Australia provides an unusually suitable setting for the identification of early canid domestication. In Eurasia, on the other hand, canid remains pass so indistinguishably from the "wild" type to the "domestic" type that we must seek blatant skeletal traits by which to chart the record of domestication. Such characteristics appear almost simultaneously between around 14,000 and 12,000 B.P. throughout Europe and Asia Minor, marking the rise of the Neolithic, the so-called New Stone Age, during which permanent nonnomadic settlements of human beings arose.

For what do we look when we seek the first domestic dogs? We are dealing, of course, with nothing but bones, and in our search for traits associated with domestication we must make detailed comparisons between large numbers of wild and domestic dogs to establish suitable criteria. Most important of these criteria are those relating to tooth rows. As we have seen, wolves raised under domestication, which do not spend their lives in the actual killing of prey, tend to show shorter muzzles and more crowded teeth than do those living in the wild. In domesticated dogs this is even truer; generations of selection for moderately peaceable relations between man and dog within human society have resulted in marked jaw changes—changes that are clear in the many dog skeletons remaining from the Neolithic of Eurasia.

One accurate measurement of the jaw changes resulting from domestication may be had by developing a ratio between the width of the roof of the mouth and the length of the upper row of teeth; generally, the larger this number the more "domesticated" the animal. Yet another measurement is the orbital angle, an indication of the development of the cheekbone and thus the power of the musculature operating the jaw. The orbital angle is that between a line drawn flat across the top of the skull and another drawn from top to

---

Two characteristics serving to distinguish domesticated from wild canid skulls are the ratio between the width of the roof of the mouth and the length of the upper row of teeth (W/L) and the orbital angle (OA).

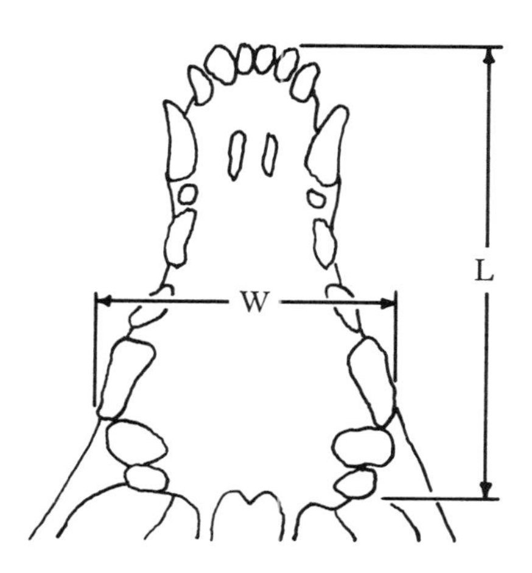

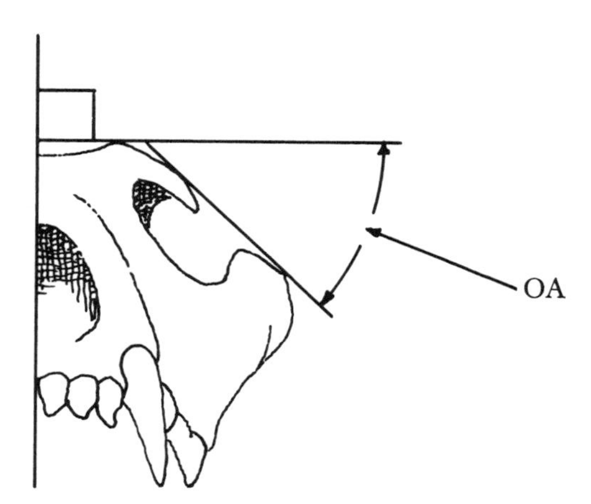

bottom of the orbit, or eye socket. In wolves, with their powerful and fully developed jaws, this angle is smaller than that in domestic dogs, whose cheekbones are less massive as a result of easy living and long genetic selection.

At any rate, by 12,000 B.P. or so, at least four recognizable subspecies of domestic dogs are identifiable in Eurasia, each of which reflects a long period of domestication and structural change. As is so often the case in classifications of the highly variable genus *Canis*, there are several ways of grouping these races; here we will refer to them mainly in terms of location, size, and apparent function within the human context, for already human beings were selecting specialized races of dogs for different tasks.

Skeletally rather like the modern huskies and other polar dogs (the wolflike breeds with erect ears and usually straight, wild-type hair) is the race *Canis familiaris inostranzewi*, apparently a working dog (sledge puller or the like) living a life like that of its modern polar counterparts and found mainly in the north of Europe and in western Asia. Two distinct breeds of such dogs have been found at Maglemose, Denmark, their bones dated by radiocarbon to about 10,000 B.P. Another primordial breed was *C. f. intermedius*, a medium-sized dog widespread through Europe, especially in the famous lake dwellings of Switzerland. A dingo- or pariahlike breed, *C. f. matris-optimae*, appears to have resembled modern sheepdogs and may itself have been a herder; a dog of this type, found in the Mount Carmel caves in Israel, has been dated to 10,800 B.P., and another, in Persia, to 11,480 B.P. The Seckenberg dog from Frankfurt-am-Main, found with the skeleton of an aurochs (the extinct wild ox from which most domesticated cattle are descended), also appears to be of this type; pollen dating has fixed the time of its death at around 11,000 B.P. Finally, there is the little *C. f. palustris*, apparently a true housedog, from which such small modern breeds as terriers may ultimately be descended.

The Europeans who first invaded the American continents found at least twenty breeds of domestic dogs sharing the ranges of the indigenous peoples from north of the Arctic Circle to Tierra del Fuego. The earliest dog remains found in the Americas are from Idaho, and they date from 10,000 B.P.; they are of a medium-sized, lightly built breed, perhaps showing a bit of coyote admixture. The earliest Americans, crossing the now-submerged Bering land bridge between 15,000 and 20,000 years ago, were superb hunters who themselves likely shared (unwittingly or purposefully) their catches with the wolves of the North American landmass. Although they left no trace of their own dealings with dogs, we may guess from the great variety of breeds present when Columbus arrived in the New World that the early hunters had lost no time in selecting from wolves those specimens best suited to their purposes. So swiftly did these hunters bring about the extinction of larger American mammals, not only elephants and giant sloths but also such modern-type herbivores as camels and horses, that it is extremely likely that they employed hunter-herder dogs to round up prey for them. At any rate, by the time of the European invasion, camels and horses were extinct and Indians maintained dogs primarily as food and beasts of burden.

In retrospect, we can see that the domestication of dogs was a gradual process beginning with a mutual hunting alliance and culminating in the isolation of a variety of distinct working breeds worldwide by about 10,000 B.P. By that time, agricultural societies based on symbioses with domesticated grasses and other plants were springing up in Asia Minor, Southeast Asia, and Central America. Such societies, with their settled ways and surpluses of food, offered humans new opportunities for specialization—as farmers, herdsmen, craftsmen, priests, soldiers, members of governing classes, and the like. With the rise of these new occupations for people came new applications for dogs, and the immense natural variability of canid types offered a multitude of avenues by which dogs might fill these roles.

We may be reasonably certain that domestic dogs arose from various wolf subspecies originally present in the areas where domestication took place. For instance, both the dogs of ancient Asia Minor and North Africa (pariah dogs) and those of dingo type seem to have arisen from the Arab (*Canis lupus arabs*) and southern Asian (*C. l. pallipes*) wolves, while larger shepherd dogs may have derived from polar-type dogs descended from the northern wolf (*C. l. lupus*, the "type" of the species). There may also have been minor admixture of other species of genus *Canis*, for as we have seen, all of these will interbreed readily. Golden jackals, for instance, are often cited as ancestors of domestic dogs, most notably by the great ethologist Konrad Lorenz. The jackal admixture must have been tenuous at best, however, for wolves and domestic dogs share the same number of chromosomes, while the jackal has an extra pair. In addition, the jackal's oddly narrow head, the animal's strange howling voice, and its strong markings are not characteristic of most domestic dogs, and even Lorenz has in recent years modified his jackal theory to conform to the greater evidence in favor of a wolf ancestor. Still, as we will see, jackals and other wild canids may have played their parts in the founding of some breeds.

In tracing the rise from shrewlike insectivores of the Carnivora, then the occurrence of various wild canids, asocial and social, and at last the appearance of the domestic dog from wolf ancestors, we have been examining the process of adaptive radiation as it results from natural selection. This is a slow process, extending in this case over many tens of millions of years. With the founding of a symbiosis between human beings and canids, however, a new form of evolution—one resulting from artificial selection—took its place. Within only 15,000 years or so of full domestication, the original wolf stocks have produced more than two hundred highly distinctive races of *Canis familiaris*, many of which are so different in form one from another that some individuals are no longer capable of interbreeding without the aid of artificial insemination. The very temperament and intelligence of dogs may also be manipulated through selective breeding; the ancient sight-hunting nervous gazehounds, for example, specialized to the chase in open country, share little in temperament with the wise and attentive shepherd dogs or the slavish spaniels and setters.

Breeds of dogs originate as living tools for human use, and in order to survive, these tools must fit their applications precisely. As raw genetic material for the fabrication of such tools, the wolf was ideal. Of all canids, wolves are seemingly the most generalized in form, therefore the most adaptable within the context of their social-hunter nature. Their domestication may be envisioned as a process of sieving, during which certain complexes of genes were isolated by artificial backbreeding to "fix" desirable forms.

As an example, consider the genes that modify coat color in dogs. As a predator, the wolf enjoys a coat coloring that permits him to blend in with a variety of backgrounds, lessening his visibility to prey animals. Each outer guard hair of a wolf is banded with up to five stripes of color, giving him an overall coloring that is somewhat hard to describe—most people call it "gray." These bands, of white, red, brown, and black, offer the wolf the indistinct outline and shading that permit him a measure of "invisibility" when he stands still against a wilderness background of snow or mottled vegetation and earth.

Domestic dogs, of course, come in a wide variety of colors, from the coal-black of the Labrador retriever through the red of the Irish setter to the pure white of the Samoyed. In addition, there are many common color *patterns*—black-and-tan, blue-tick, black-and-white, and the like—all the result of human selection for same. In modern times we have learned something of the mechanisms governing the inheritance of coloring in dogs, and have established a sort of genetic shorthand to describe it.

Geneticists have dubbed dog-coloring genes the A Series, and have isolated a dominance pattern according to which, if dogs of two colors are mated, one of these colors is more likely to appear in their offspring. Coal-black, a^s in the shorthand, is dominant over a^y, red (including colors from pure Irish setter red to black-red or sable). The a^y gene is in turn dominant over the wolf-coat (wild-type) coloring, a^w, which appears to variable degrees in such domestic breeds as huskies, Norwegian elkhounds, German shepherds, and the like. Again, the a^w gene dominates the coding for the black-and-tan (bicolor) gene, a^t, in which the upper part of the body is typically black, embellished with reddish-tan markings inside the ears and above the eyes, and red below; such coloring is typical of Doberman pinschers and bloodhounds, among many others.

There are countless other genes, recessive ones, that alter the A Series; for example, the breeding with a black dog of a dog with a recessive gene dubbed *ee* will change black to red in their offspring; again, the recessive *bb* changes black to a liver color of the sort common in weimaraners and some dachshunds.

Other genetic patterns govern hair length (short dominates long), coat texture (smooth dominates coarse), and even the pattern of spotting in black-and-white sheepdogs, Dalmatians, and others. Innumerable other genes govern such characteristics as skeletal form, ear shape (lop-ears dominate over erect ears, which are comparatively uncommon in domestic breeds), and the less definable behavioral aspects of different strains that result in such specialized activities as pointing, setting, retrieving, sheepherding, and the patterns of prey chasing in greyhounds and carriage following in Dalmatians.

Withal, each breed of domestic dog originated as a useful subset of the possibilities of the original wolf, with a corresponding minimization of other wolf characteristics in accordance with the design at hand. That loving terrier, in other words, is a fraction of a wolf—delightful, but a fraction, nonetheless, of the old wolf potential. As an illustration of this important fact, brain size in wolf-sized domestic dogs is often as much as 20 percent smaller than that in wolves themselves!

EARLY PHYLOGENY OF DOMESTIC BREEDS

In the study of animal evolution, we find that most forms display relationships that occur in a classic "family tree" pattern, with various adaptive radiations appearing as branchings in their evolutionary lines. Within the context of domestic forms, however, the artificially produced adaptive radiations are far more complex; here the many backbreedings and crossings between races produce family histories that are more "netlike" than "treelike." Breeds of dogs may be crossed again after long isolation to produce new breeds, then these with still others. Such a process can only obscure the past history of the animals under consideration, making the task of tracing dog evolution a complicated one at best. Still, there are several broad ancestral types of domestic dogs. Each of these, embracing many distinctive breeds, enables us to gain a useful handle on the dog story despite the whimsical intervention of human beings.

As we have seen, the early domestication of the dog resulted in the isolation of several more or less distinct breeds by about 11,000 years ago. In modern times, we still see a number of "primitive" domestic breeds throughout Eurasia, northern Africa, and Australasia—breeds representing fundamental man-dog symbioses that have persisted virtually unchanged through millennia. Perhaps the best known of these are the so-called polar dogs, the rather wolflike breeds originally sharing the ranges of the nomadic peoples

---

A polar sampler, showing (a) a malamute, (b) a Samoyed, (c) an akita, the Japanese hunting dog, (d) a chow, (e) a schipperke, and (f) a Maltese dwarf. All share in appearance much of the character of their wolf ancestors.

a
b
c
d
e
f

inhabiting roughly the areas enclosed by the Arctic Circle. Like wolves, most of these dogs have banded guard hairs and consequently "wild" coloring, erect ears, heavy coats, broad and powerful long-snouted skulls framed by display ruffs, robust trotting builds, and an air of jolly independence. Most wolfish among them are the huskies and the malamutes; these breeds, domesticated by nomads as hunting and sledge dogs, are in their native habitats commonly backbred intentionally to wolves (by tying bitches in heat where dog wolves are sure to find them) to retain their characteristic sturdiness in adversity, for they inhabit the "rim of the world" and must be strong and independent to survive the rigors of their environment.

Human beings and wolves have shared taiga (boreal forest) and tundra habitats since before the glaciers last receded, and the resultant semidomesticated dogs took on several new forms around the North Pole as the symbiosis persisted during the nomads' ceaseless wanderings. By Neolithic times, several varieties of polar dogs had appeared in response to the increasing applications being developed by the men of those times for their canid allies. In addition to huskies (Norwegian and Siberian, as well as the Alaskan malamutes), the polar group includes such widespread breeds as Samoyeds, the all-white dogs of the Samoyed people of Siberia, and Norwegian elkhounds, the ancient wolflike Viking hunting dogs. Samoyed dogs have been further bred into midget as well as full-sized forms, perhaps originally in response to the ever-present need for footwarmers in those cold climes.

In addition to sledge pullers of the husky type, hunters and "cutters" similar to modern German shepherd dogs appear in remnants of Neolithic settlements. Each of these was the result of selection of characteristics strongly typical of wild wolves, and their appearance remains to this day clearly wolfish in spite of the intervening millennia of artificial genetic manipulation. During the Neolithic the sheepdog, too, made its first appearance, as such herbivores as goats and sheep came under domestication. Along with such ancient breeds as the Scandinavian elkhounds, these sheepherders suggest some admixture of nonpolar type at an early date, reflecting the migration into northern lands of groups of peoples from more southerly climes such as those of Asia Minor.

In the same manner the polar genes moved south; apparently the Maltese dogs of the Mediterranean region are dwarfed polar dogs, as are the Pomeranians of Central Europe. Similarly dwarfed are the keeshonds, the canal dogs of the Netherlands; except for its long hair and smaller size, the keeshond is almost indistinguishable from an elkhound. Another such is the spitz (which means "pointed"—the characteristic muzzle shape of the breed) in all its many forms; in fact, "spitz" is a name often applied to the polar group as a whole. In

Central Asia and China, chows represent the selective breeding of Samoyed-type polar dogs for food and for the luxuriant fur typical of the group. Chows are red in coat and oddly endowed with blue-black mucosa of the mouth, a genetic trait selected from ancient times. The sculpted "lion-dogs" at the gates to Chinese temples are stylized chows; real ones, resembling lions in their red-gold coloring and facial ruffs, originally functioned as temple guards.

Another ancient group of dogs, represented by the aforementioned dingoes of Australia and the pariah dogs of southern Asia and northern Africa, reflects the long-standing symbiosis between human beings of these regions and the indigenous southern wolves *Canis lupus pallipes* (the southern Asian wolf) and *C. l. arabs* (the Arab wolf). Both of these wolf subspecies are somewhat smaller and less heavily furred than their relatives of the north, and the domestic dogs descended from them share their comparatively light builds and short fur.

Pariah dogs are short-haired animals of medium size that generally live an inquilinistic (tenant) life among the societies of India, Asia Minor, and northern Africa; here, while sharing the very cities of men, they occupy a unique social niche in which they function as scavengers while remaining otherwise undomesticated (the word *pariah* derives from a southern Indian word meaning "drummer" and was applied to the lowest social castes of the region—those who were too mean in status to serve as warriors and were relegated in battle to the beating of drums; by extension, *pariah* has come to be applied to any people or animals—vultures and dogs and the like—that live by scavenging the refuse of their betters). Still, pariah dogs are definitely descended from early domesticated forms; in their short, variegated coats and curly tails, they show every sign of selective breeding at some remote date.

The pariah dog (*left*) is as highly variable in coloring as are most other domestic dogs.

Their variable breeding pattern—two or more heats per year instead of the single breeding season characteristic of wild canids—is also a domestic trait. On the other hand, pariahs do move in packs ordered much like those of wolves, in some places exerting considerable predatory pressure on both wild herbivores and domestic stock.

The domesticated ancestors of pariah dogs were probably herd dogs sharing almost nothing of the family lives of their human allies. As game became more scarce and agricultural symbioses with grasses were begun by human beings in Asia Minor, some such dogs seem to have lost their initial usefulness as herders and been abandoned. Ultimately, many of the peoples of Asia Minor and India came to regard dogs as ecologic competitors, for they eat almost anything humans eat, and only in societies possessing an abundance of extra food can a man-dog symbiosis persist. Thus the pariah inherited his outcast status at an early date, and that status is reflected in many early writings of the pastoral peoples of his range. Both Hindus and Muslims have traditionally regarded dogs as unclean, and the ancient Hebrews went so far as to call the eating of canine flesh "an abomination." Even today, pariah dogs commonly devour excrement and corpses and all the rest of the detritus produced by human societies, and they are frequently offered water in recognition of their activities as cleansers of the streets.

Almost indistinguishable (and likely descended) from a pariah-dingo type is the famous basenji dog of North Africa, one of the oldest pure breeds in existence. Like wild canids, adult basenjis will not bark unless taught to do so by other domestic breeds. His silence has earned the basenji a place as a game-flusher among African peoples south to the Equator, to whom the breed spread by way of Nilotic trade routes in ancient times. The basenji is a small dog (about 10 kilograms), reflecting selection for midget size; it was early favored as a housepet and was the first to be depicted in Egyptian art—basenjis appear in household scenes dating from about 5000 B.P.

With the diminishing availability of easily captured game animals in Neolithic times arose a need for very swift domestic dogs to aid in the capture of such fleet creatures as antelope. Thus arose, possibly from pariah-dingo stock, yet a third ancient group, the sight-hunters, or gazehounds. These, selected by their human allies for speed in crossing open country, represent the earliest sharp physical departure from the ancestral wolf form; whereas wolves, polar dogs, and pariah-dingo types hunt by tireless running in groups, the gazehounds capture their prey by sprinting madly across the grasslands in nonfamilial pairs or platoons, using their eyes rather than the old canid intelligence and social proclivities. In hunting with gazehounds, prey is first sighted by human beings and only then are the dogs released for the chase. So

The basenji is an ancient North African race of small pariah type.

excitable are these dogs that they are often hooded like hawks in falconry until prey is started from concealment.

The golden jackal may have played a part in the founding of this complex of domesticated breeds. Jackals are very narrow-headed and lightly built compared to wolves, and are also preadapted to the warm open savannas and deserts of Asia Minor and northern Africa. Gazehounds, although varying from one another in both color and coat length, are almost uniformly long-legged, narrow-headed, and lightly built. Jackals were probably recognized early as superb warm-weather coursers in their own right, and perhaps some of their adaptations for such hunting were crossed into a pariahlike type to produce such breeds as the saluki of Asia Minor, probably the oldest existing purebred dog. Ancient Egyptian paintings depict a variety of greyhound-type breeds, and the very name *greyhound* is said to be a derivative of the archaic *gazehound*.

Gazehounds possess a distinctive dolichocephalic (long-headed) profile with an unusual convex nose line, produced by great development of the nasal cavities and frontal sinuses. This characteristic facial aspect is a result of selection for exaggeration of the cooling mechanisms in such speedy animals, for, as we have seen, much of the brain-cooling equipment in canids is based on movement of air over the evaporative surfaces contained within the nose. In addition, the chests of coursers are deep and spacious, further reflecting both the need for increased cooling efficiency and the increased oxygen requirement of these consummate sprinters.

Allied to the specialized character of gazehound physiology is their unique skeletal structure, a framework departing sharply in form from that of more wolflike forms and approaching that of the antelope and other swift prey for which the gazehounds were originally bred. Wolves and their like run on stout, heavily muscled legs, their spines flexing moderately in time with the rhythm of their running. Gazehounds, on the other hand, concentrate their running musculature in their upper legs and lower backs, excess mass in the lower legs having been bred out in consideration of lightness. Rather than in a gallop like that of wolves, the gazehound runs in an almost rabbitlike series of rapidly sequential leaps, its series of lumbar (lower-back) vertebrae flexing and unflexing like a steel leaf spring. These vertebrae, wider than those of other canids, support and are worked by mighty loin muscles whose action results in the "curling-and-uncurling" sprint characteristic of these lightning-fast dogs, some of which can cover 60 kilometers per hour.

As a sight-hunting form, the gazehound (not, incidentally, to be confused with the scent-hound) is endowed with exceptionally good eyesight. In all gazehounds, the eyes are large and may even seem to protrude from the head. In connection with the sight-hunting function, gazehounds have been bred to exhibit a "chasing" response to any rapidly moving object. This response, present in all canids to some extent, is so strong in gazehounds that, as I mentioned earlier, the animals are often hooded until prey is sighted lest they set off after a horseman or some other such inappropriate "prey."

The need for speedy dogs was widespread in ancient times, and gazehounds were adopted and modified by many Eurasian peoples. Greyhounds of the Egyptian type were common throughout the Mediterranean region in ancient times, their pictures having always been popular among artistic folk of the classical world. In more northerly Europe, the Celts bred gazehound blood into their deerhounds and wolfhounds, shaggy breeds of large size that

---

A gazehound sampler. *Above*: the saluki, perhaps the oldest of surviving breeds; *middle*: the greyhound, racer *par excellence*; *below*: the strange face of the Afghan hound.

were often used in war as well as to capture alive such fast prey as deer and wolves. In central and western Russia the borzoi, or "Russian wolfhound," is the characteristic gazehound; other than in possessing longer hair, it is simply a large greyhound of the Mediterranean type. Miniature greyhounds were bred by the Greeks and Romans for use in hunting rabbits; their descendants live on in the Italian greyhounds of modern times. Perhaps the newest gazehound is the whippet, a British breed of small size established during the nineteenth century as a "poor man's racehorse."

While the racing of greyhounds and whippets is probably the typical modern employment of gazehound stock, Arabs still employ salukis and Afghan hounds (a large version of the saluki) in the hunting of antelope. Gazehound genes also figure in the background of the venerable collies, sheep dogs of various types in whom speed is valued as an accessory in the control of large flocks. Collies are of mixed polar-gazehound background and are ideal for working in the cold climates of northwestern Europe, where they originated during Roman times. Various midget races of collies (Shetland sheepdogs,

The whippet exhibits all of the typical gazehound traits: large eyes, long legs, deep chest, and arched lower back.

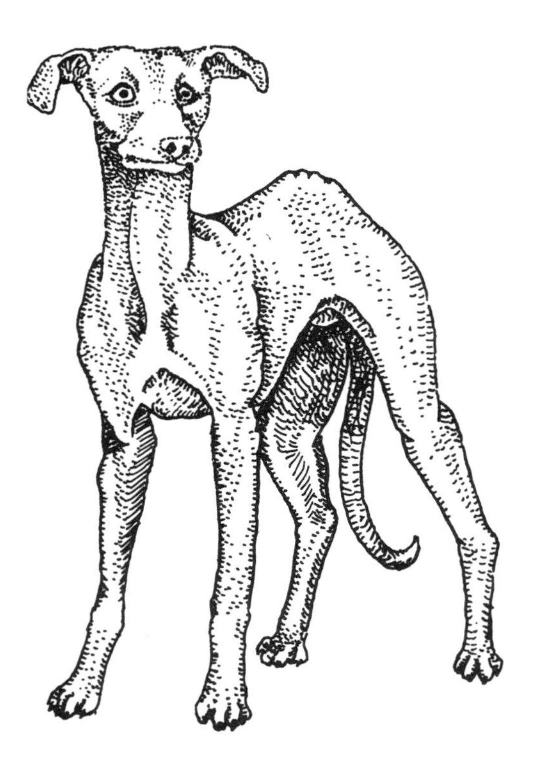

The two original collies, short-haired (*left*) and long-haired, both show strong gazehound admixture.

Welsh sheepdogs, and other collielike breeds worldwide) have traveled wherever the wool-gathering British have established their herds of sheep.

Significantly, the only dogs that have ever bitten me are gazehounds. I am one who enjoys running and, in my years of doing so, have twice been attacked by such dogs, one a greyhound and one an Afghan. The most ferocious guard dogs, the most neurotic toy dogs—none of these has ever offered me more than a good deal of bluff; but in both my experiences with dogbite, the sight of a large running animal was too much for the gazehounds to resist. Such is the extent to which the temperament of a higher mammal may be

The Irish wolfhound is an ancient breed of shaggy polar admixture with some gazehound ancestry.

manipulated by genetic selection! On the other hand, aficionados of salukis and Afghan hounds in New Mexico have learned the sport of coursing these beautiful animals after the formidable jackrabbit, the very epitome of velocity in the semiarid highlands. In jackrabbits may be had all of the essentials of the ancient sport of coursing (a word derived from the Latin *cursus*, "running"), and the sight of a jackrabbit hunt with gazehounds is one of the most exciting available in this tame age.

MASTIFFS

The polar, pariah-dingo, and gazehound dogs probably represent the earliest attempts by human beings to adjust the forms of animals to their own specialized needs. Reflecting human intervention mainly in their outward forms and coats, these early races still share with wolves a general conformation and (in most cases) size that bespeak comparatively little departure from the wolf physique and capability. All of them probably originated as races well over 8,000 years ago, and all survive either through their continuing applicability to human needs or through their ability to return to a feral state while retaining the signs of their man-altered ancestry.

By the time of the rise of the first real city-states, however, increasing leisure for human beings began to reflect itself in the evolution of economic classes of people unconnected with the collection and distribution of food, these functions having gradually been relegated to specialized agricultural workers—farmers and herdsmen. Those released from food production invented new occupations, and hereditary classes of priests and governors, bureaucrats and craftsmen began appearing in bewildering numbers. With them came new forms of dogs, dogs as little resembling their wolf ancestors as did the new societies resemble preagricultural hunter-gatherer tribes. As grain-based prosperity increased, surpluses of food permitted the keeping of dogs whose functions were no longer strictly related to the hunt or other work. Ever variable, the canid stock offered wide choices of mutations, whose visible results have always fascinated us.

The forces of natural selection, ever vigilant, selected for efficiency among canids for millions of years. Sharp deviation from the form and behavior necessary for the canid way of life was fatal; hence the generally homogeneous aspect of wild canids throughout the world. Within the new context of artificial selection, however, monsters—human, animal, or plant—have always been sources of interest to human beings. The fascination survives, as witness the freak show in any modern carnival; but in ancient times the unexpected occurrence of a mutant, a monster born of apparently normal parents, was cause for great concern. Supernatural intervention was the cause attributed to the conception of such freaks, and thus strange mutant dogs became highly valued by their owners. Of course, by definition domesticated animals and plants descend from mutants selected by human beings whose attention was attracted to the sudden appearance of strange characteristics in such organisms. Nowhere is this process more apparent than in the evolution of the hundreds of modern breeds of dogs from their ancestors among the polar, pariah-dingo, and gazehound families.

Among the commonest mutations to appear in higher vertebrates are those relating to overall body size. Gigantism or dwarfism occurs spontaneously in about 1 of every 10,000 births, both canid and human. One of the greatest and most distinctive lineages of dogs is that among whose ancestors some form of hereditary gigantism appeared perhaps 10,000 years ago. Such gigantism is usually related to the growth hormone–producing pituitary gland, a nodule of tissue located beneath the brain and, in wolves and dogs of similar size, weighing about .065 gram. Giant dogs, in which the pituitary may weight twice as much, first appear in the historical record primarily as beasts of war and sentinels. These giants seem to have originated in northern India or Tibet, perhaps from large mountain wolves of the race *Canis lupus laniger* with an admixture of dingo-type genes from the pariah race. Presumably, herdsmen of the north of India spent centuries selecting for size in their shepherd dogs. These dogs, whose function it is to protect domestic animals from predation by wolves and other wild animals (as well as by human thieves), must at once be differentiated from sheepdogs, the latter being herders—agile, responsive, observant. Sheepdogs *herd* flocks; shepherd dogs *protect* them.

In addition to possessing a protective tendency, shepherd dogs must be at least as large and powerful as are the predators against whom they protect their stupid herbivorous charges. Initially, selection for size from among the normal variations within litters (influenced, no doubt, by a generous admixture of wolf genes) permitted the isolation of shepherds from the northern

An acromegalic human being with his acromegalic dog (Tibetan mastiff). Note in each the large size, heavy limbs, and enlargement of the bones and flesh of the face.

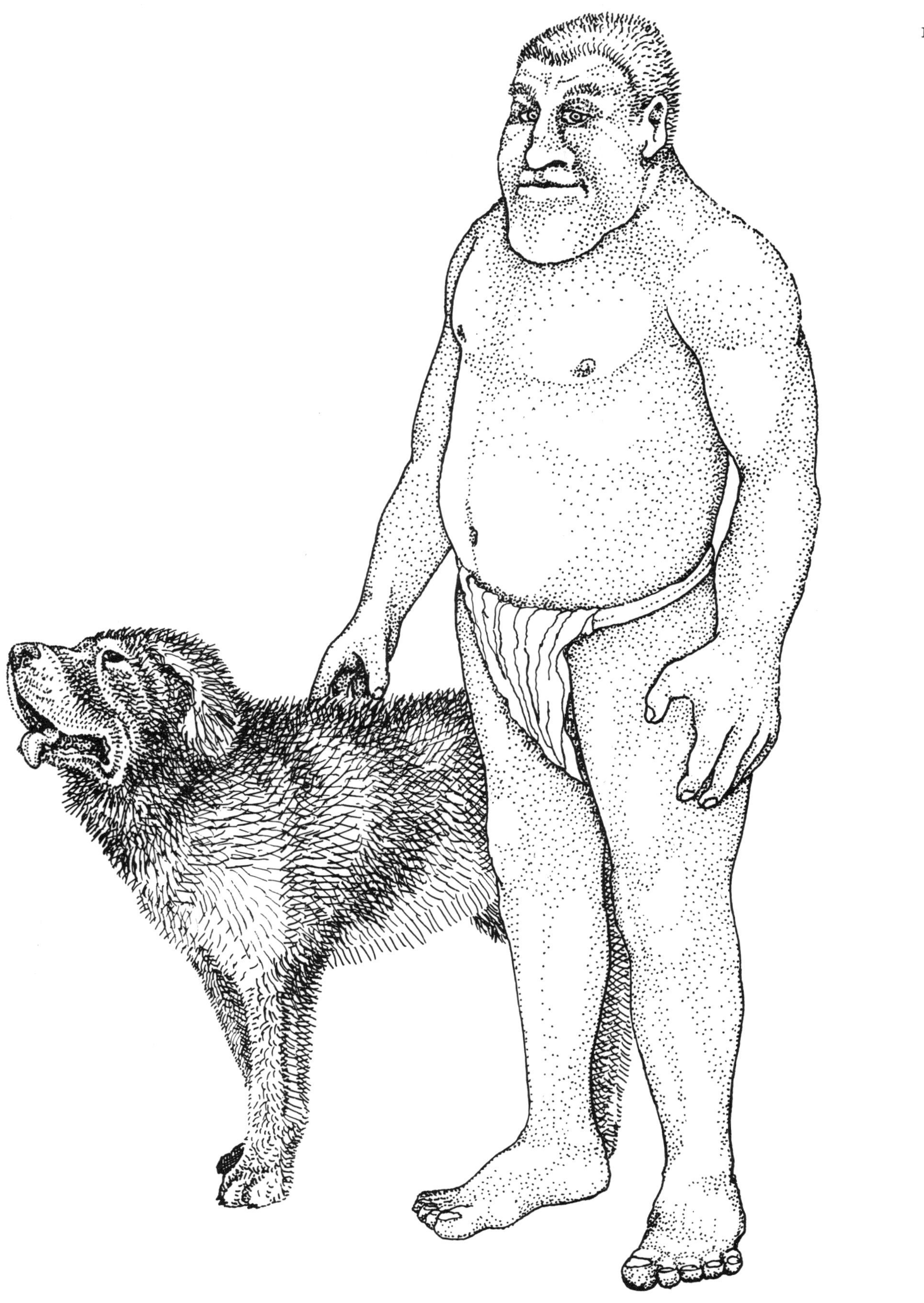

Indian mountain-dog stock, much as this was accomplished in Europe from polar stock. At some point, however, a puppy was born with a mutant gene, probably one coding for the common form of gigantism that we call acromegaly (hugeness of the extremities).

Acromegaly is a disturbance of the pituitary which causes the gland to produce excess growth hormone. Because it is a fairly common mutation as such things go, it must occur as frequently among wild wolves as among domestic dogs. Unfortunately, acromegaly is a condition affecting the entire physiology, producing changes that are not at all suited to the life-style of wild canids; it is, in short, selected against in nature. Under domestication, however, acromegalic dogs had a multitude of uses from the start. Acromegalics are literally huge, weighing as much as 100 kilograms (and sometimes more!), as contrasted with the normal canid upper size limit of about 60 kilograms. In isolating strains of acromegalic dogs, early herdsmen discovered quite a new animal, a form so very large as to discourage most opposition by mass alone.

Acromegaly produces characteristic changes in appearance apart from size. The bones of the extremities, the limbs and feet, are unusually massive, and so, consequently, are the muscles that operate them. Moreover, the face undergoes specific changes as the dog (or human, for that matter) afflicted with acromegaly achieves maturity. The flesh about the face—especially the lips, cheeks, and ears—grows out of proportion to the skull, producing a characteristic wrinkly, jowly appearance; in dogs, the ears hang beside the head and flap about loosely. The lower jaw also tends to exceed in growth the rest of the skull, so that a heaviness of the mouth regions (and great biting power) becomes apparent early in the growth process. The bones of the cheeks and those surrounding the eyes continue to grow after the braincase has achieved maximum size, typically producing in acromegalic dogs a fearsome expression that was early applied in the use of these giants as guard dogs for the emerging agricultural settlements.

Once strains of giant dogs were isolated in the north of India, they became coveted items of trade throughout the ancient world. Assyrian sculpture dating from around 3000 B.P. shows war dogs almost identical in appearance to the modern mastiffs that are descended from them. Proceeding ever westward along the trading routes of the Mediterranean peoples, these dogs were treasured and further bred by the Greeks, who called them Molossians (after the ancient district of Molossia in Epirus, northwestern Greece), and by the Romans, who gave the group its modern name, mastiff (from *mansuetus*, "tame," referring to their use of these giants as family guard dogs).

By the time of Christ, mastiffs were a common sight throughout the civilized world. Originally short-coated, as were their pariah-type ancestors, some were crossed with dogs of polar type to produce the shaggy mastiffs we know today as Saint Bernards, Great Pyrenees, and the like; others, finding their way east, seem to have been mixed there with northern dogs, to leave traces in the fleshy-faced but normal-sized chows. Introduced to the British Isles by Phoenicians, Celts, and Roman legionaries, mastiffs survive almost

Typical mastiffs include the short-haired English mastiff (*above*) and the white, long-haired Great Pyrenees.

unchanged in the modern breed of that name as well as in several other uniquely British strains that we will examine later. Indeed, in all the larger dogs (and many small ones to boot) traces of acromegaly survive today in the form of extra skin about the face, heavy limbs, and abnormally mighty jaws.

Gigantism does, however, have its disadvantages. The modern giants—the Saint Bernards, Great Danes and Pyrenees, British mastiffs, Newfoundlands, and those of mixed gazehound-mastiff stock such as Irish wolfhounds and Scottish deerhounds—are among the shortest-lived of canid races. Such dogs are susceptible to intestinal obstruction, for instance, due to the inability of their intestinal mesenteries to support the sheer weight of their guts. Also, these dogs succumb early to heart attacks, back and hind-leg problems, hip dysplasia, and troubles with chewing brought on by the typical anomalies of their jaws. While a normal-sized dog may live up to (and sometimes beyond) two decades, giants rarely survive ten years.

Such short lives are indeed a pity, for the long working history of mastiffs has resulted in selection for intelligence and loyalty unequaled in many smaller breeds. Famed for their protective and loving dispositions, Newfoundland and Saint Bernard mastiffs originated as rescue dogs that cheerfully braved the terrible conditions of their respective Canadian and Alpine winters. As guard dogs, mastiffs are admired above all for their discrimination; a good mastiff can examine an intruder with such care that he need not bark at once, but will follow the interloper, watching him and warning with a rumbling growl should he transgress the limits taught the mastiff by his master. And if a thief ignores such warning, the dog may simply seize him and sit on him, baying for the master to come deal with him in the custom appropriate to human beings.

Throughout history, mastiffs have accompanied their masters to war, often wearing armor and even leather-mounted knives to damage the legs of the enemy and his horses. In cavalry engagements, some mastiffs were fitted with torches mounted on their armor, the fire of which frightened horses and thus disrupted charges before they happened. Mastiffs cheerfully attacked the elephant-mounted archers of classical times, frightening the pachyderms into disarray and confounding the designs of those who employed them. As hunters, mastiffs have long been employed against such formidable beasts as lions and wolves, and as shepherd dogs, of course, they know no equal. Modern shepherd mastiffs include the white Great Pyrenees (which originated, as its name suggests, in the mountainous Basque regions separating the Iberian peninsula from the rest of Europe) and the great Eastern European shepherds called komondors and Kuvasczok. Basque fishermen took mastiff-type

A doggy knight in chain and plate. This medieval animal charged cavalry to frighten and disrupt the horses.

dogs to Maritime Canada, and from them originated the black Newfoundland sea-rescue dogs.

An important offshoot of the acromegalic line resulted in the isolation not less than 5,000 years ago of the bloodhound, or scent-hound (to be carefully distinguished from the gazehound, discussed earlier). The original bloodhound was a mastiff-type weighing about 60 kilograms. Lighter in build than many of its giant ancestors (a difference due to selection for tireless running), the bloodhound reflects its ancestry in a typically acromegalic face with "too much skin," hanging jowls, and long, floppy ears. Originating in Tibet or northern India with the rest of the mastiffs, the bloodhound was selected from the start with one particular factor in mind, the ability to trace scents.

As a tracker, the bloodhound knows no equal. Presented with the scent of identical twins, a bloodhound can distinguish the two and follow one or the other, according to instructions. The origin of bloodhounds reflects a bit of the underside of human behavior, for these (very gentle, incidentally) ani-

The bloodhound, whose fleshy face represents acromegaly in the extreme, is a sniffer *par excellence*. His extraordinary nose, capable of distinguishing even the scents of identical twins, is a result of ancient man's need to track escaped slaves.

---

mals seem to have been bred to track escaped slaves. Bloodhounds do not attack those whom they trail; in ancient times this was left to other mastiffs, which followed their bloodhound cousins in the hunt.

In conjunction with the tracking function, the ancestral bloodhound was designed with handler contact in mind. Hence the "bell," the unique howling cry of the scent-hound group as a whole, designed to enable pursuing men to determine the direction of the chase. The tracking function is also reflected in the hound's tireless activity; he can—indeed, *must*—run as long as he stays awake. He is not particularly fast as dogs go, having been designed as a pursuer of the slower *Homo sapiens*, but run he does, seemingly forever. So specialized as trackers are they that bloodhounds and their derivative breeds are good for little else. This hyperspecialization has resulted in a measure of stupidity (hound-lovers would call it single-minded tenacity) unequaled in the canid world. Hounds run and snuffle, snuffle and run, and do precious little else. Even the characteristic fidelity of dogs is attenuated in these breeds, which adopt new masters with much the ease other dogs show in adopting new foods.

Once this consummate tracker came into being, he was used in the founding of scores of other breeds whose functions centered on scent tracking. Although they come in all sizes from miniature to huge, scent-hounds reflect their acromegalic origins in their dangling ears and characteristically fleshy faces. Small hounds such as the highly specialized dachshunds (badger-

The beagle (*above*) and black-and-tan coonhound represent specialized branches of scent-hound stock selected for specific prey; the beagle is the consummate rabbit-hound, while the coonhound was "invented" by European colonists enamored of the raccoon's tasty flesh and fighting spirit.

---

hounds) result from a strong admixture of dwarfing genes into the original stock; the basset, the perfect rabbithound, with his acromegalic head, heavy body, and tiny legs, is ideally designed for crashing through briars in search of the elusive lagopine prey. The many newer breeds, notably the coon-hounds of the Americas (blue-tick, black-and-tan, and others), share in the generally acromegalic faces of their bloodhound ancestry while sporting lighter bodies in response to the requirement that they cover vast distances in a short time. Thus also the foxhounds (American and British), the harriers, and other running hounds—all of which may share a bit of ancient gazehound admixture in their genetic makeup.

Also derived from an acromegalic bloodhound ancestry, although highly variable in size and form, are the many breeds today called sporting dogs. Bearing the ancient mastiff stamp in their fleshy jowls and dangling ears, these include pointers, setters, spaniels, and retrievers, as well as the ancient chariot dogs from which are descended the modern Dalmatians, or coach dogs. The latter, originally selected to accompany charioteers and to clear other war dogs from the path of the horses, persist today as pets and as mascots to fire companies; so specialized are they that it can truly be said that Dalmatians love wheeled vehicles, often becoming inveterate chasers of cars. There are strains of Dalmatians that run beneath the axles of carriages, strains that run in front of carriages, strains that run beside carriages, and strains that ride on carriages. Each strain is strictly hereditary, a fact testifying abundantly to the almost incredible governing effect that heredity can have on behavior.

Pointers originated as spotting-dogs, animals designed to locate prey by scent so that human beaters might drive it into the open to be captured by archers, trained cheetahs, gazehounds, or hawks. Pointers are an ancient group, whose portraits appear from the days of ancient Egypt. Wolves, on discovering small, concealed prey, often freeze in midstep until their cohorts flush the prey. Artificial selection for this behavior resulted in the pointer's "point," a characteristic physical position of readiness that does not, through the magic of breeding, follow through into a true attack.

Most European spaniels (from the French *espagnol*, "Spanish") possess tight, wavy coats from which water is easily shaken, and they are believed to have originated from small mastiff-type dogs used by the Basques to chase and retrieve water birds. There are now water spaniels, land spaniels (known as cockers—flushers of woodcock), and springer spaniels (so called because of their use in springing concealed birds from cover). Derived from some pointer-springer cross are the setters, a comparatively new group whose function is related to the evolution of shotguns; setters "set," freezing when they locate prey and awaiting a spoken command to flush it. The various toy spaniels, by the way, derive from old Asian dwarf groups and are not part of the true sporting-dog line; thus the Japanese spaniel, Tibetan spaniel, papillon, and others, while generally included among the "real" spaniels, belong in the next chapter.

Retrievers, as the name implies, recover grounded game for their masters. Many also set or point, and thus make superb all-around gundogs as well as useful Seeing Eye and police workers. Typically mastifflike in face, they are

Assorted specialized descendants of mastiff stock. *From left:* a Dalmatian coachdog, a pointer, an English springer spaniel, an Irish setter, a Labrador retriever, a standard poodle.

---

well within the normal wolf range in size and thus generally long-lived and little given to medical problems. Many writers suggest that the retriever group as a whole derives some of its character from pointer and spaniel admixture with polar-type ancestry. Most likely, the Labrador retriever is derived in part from the black Newfoundland mastiff.

Poodles, the most specialized of retrievers, originated in Central Europe as *Pudelen* (German for "puddlers," or water dogs). They are famed for their intelligence and adaptability as entertainers, but today function primarily as pets. The many artificial clipping styles for poodles originate from their working past, during which these long-haired dogs accumulated large quantities of mud in their coats if left ungroomed. So popular have poodles become, that large, medium, and midget races are distributed worldwide today; their very numbers prevent the inbreeding that has all too often destroyed the character of other popular breeds.

MIDGETS AND DWARVES

Another common complex of genetic mutations results in size ranges smaller than normal. Again, this is true among canids as well as among human beings. Several different factors, environmental as well as genetic, can produce abnormally small individuals. Mere starvation of youngsters can produce small adults—this is especially so when malnutrition produces rickets, a disease characterized by abnormal growth of long bones, resulting in stunting and twisting of the limbs. Such deformations are strictly environmental in character, however; a stunted individual with average-sized parents will produce average-sized offspring, and if those offspring are given nutritious food, they will grow normally. Arising from genetic mutations, true pygmies (or midgets) pass on their small size to their offspring. Noting this, early breeders of dogs took care to select for small size, much as they did for acromegaly among the ancestral mastiffs.

(It must be admitted here that the only form of animal that makes me nervous to a high degree is a tiny dog. The emotional response most people reserve for spiders, centipedes, and other crawlers, I feel for all dogs smaller than a red fox. This prejudice cannot help but surface in my writing, and while I apologize to the owners of Pekingeses and other such monsters, I cannot change on this score without extensive psychotherapy.)

Two broad types of mutations produced the myriad tiny breeds of dogs with which the world is afflicted. The simple process of artificial selection for small size from among the variety of pups in a litter leads to few or no gross abnormalities in form. Over many generations this process results in the production of pygmies, small dogs otherwise much like their ancestors. More abrupt in its occurrence is acromegaly's opposite number, the mutation pro-

A sampler of midget dogs. *From left:* a toy Manchester terrier, a Pomeranian, a toy poodle. The cat they bother serves as scale.

---

ducing midget dogs by reason of its effect on the pituitary growth hormone. Normal in most respects, midgets simply quit growing while young, retaining as adults many infantile characters along with small size. The midgets are generally well-proportioned little animals, somewhat large of head (to accommodate a normal-sized brain) but otherwise little distorted from whatever form their progenitors took.

Most of today's midget breeds of dogs are of comparatively recent origin, having been selected from stock of normal size within the past few centuries. Thus we have miniature Doberman pinschers, toy poodles, whippets (miniature British greyhounds), assorted midget sheepdogs (such as Shetland collies), and a host of others. In addition, there are several very ancient midget breeds from various parts of the world, including Italian greyhounds, Maltese and Pomeranian dogs (miniature versions of the polar stock), papillons ("butterflies"), a sort of midget Asiatic form originally popularized for Europeans by the Flemings and French, and, from the Western Hemisphere, the smallest dog of all—the Chihuahua, the miniature Central American dog, often weighing less than a kilogram as an adult.

Mention of the Chihuahua permits us an interesting digression into the ecology of the late great Aztec civilization of old Mexico. The Aztecs lived in an unusual ecosystem supporting no large mammals suitable for domestication as food; all such animals had been killed off by earlier peoples of the area, long before the rise of the densely populated Aztec agricultural civilization. Forced to content themselves with ducks, turkeys, and domestic dogs as protein sources, the Aztecs enthusiastically bred and ate a wide assortment of comestible dogs including the famous Xoloitzcuintli, or Mexican hairless, a

Two of the midget food-dog breeds of Mexico. The larger is the Xoloitzcuintli, or Mexican hairless; the smaller is the Chihuahua, tiniest of dogs, descendant of an ancient Mexican breed that shows much modern genetic tampering. *Upper right:* a small clay sculpture of a fattened dog, a grave offering of the Colima cultural group of western Mexico. These "Colima dogs" were common furnishings of human burial sites between A.D. 800 and 1500; they reflect the dependence of the Colima culture on dogs as food both on earth and in the afterlife. This specimen is from the pre-Columbian collection of Dr. Philip Shultz of Tesuque, New Mexico.

horrible-looking naked animal that was highly prized as food by its protein-conscious breeders. The modern Chihuahua may enjoy an admixture of Asiatic midget genes, perhaps from the Chinese "crested" midget, whose hair is also extremely sparse. Chihuahuas are bred today in two races, long- and short-haired. Exhibiting the classic "Napoleon complex," these diminutive dogs are often ferocious out of all proportion to their size and therefore make excellent watchdogs.

With the possible exception of the Aztec food dogs, the midgets discussed above reflect leisure in all respects. Often aptly called "toys," most serve no real working function today except as alarm dogs, all of them sharing with the Chihuahua a rather nervous and high-strung temperament. There is, however, a large family of midget dogs "invented" specifically for the hardest sort of work; these are the terriers, originally bred as hunters of fox-sized and smaller mammals from some ancestor bearing traces of both polar and pariah-dingo genes. Terriers derive their group name from the Latin *terra,* "earth"; they literally go to earth, pursuing their prey into the very recesses of its burrow if possible. In conjunction with this trait, terriers have been selected through thousands of years for absolute fearlessness and will attack creatures many times their size with the same enthusiasm they display in killing rats. They are, in short, utilized as true killers rather than as mere hunters like most modern breeds, and terrier genes are thus predominant in most races used in the barbaric "sports" of dogfighting and animal-baiting.

Ranging in size from about 20 kilograms down to only 2, the fifty or so breeds of terriers are all characterized by the tightly muscled build typical of midgets, in conjunction with a curly or wiry coat perhaps derived in part from their polar ancestry. Some writers even classify the basenji among the terriers, although, as we have seen, the basenji is little different from the typical pariah dog. Perhaps closer to terrier ancestry is the rare pharaoh hound, an ancient Egyptian breed now confined almost entirely to Malta, where it is the national dog. The earliest representations of terrierlike dogs do indeed come from dynastic Egypt, where these dogs were probably used in conjunction with cats in the protection of grain supplies from rodents.

Still, the terriers as a modern group are centered in distribution in Western Europe. In mentioning certain small British "hunting dogs of great power and worth," the second-century Greek poet Oppian may have been referring to early terriers. Certainly, the British Isles have produced more than their share of terriers and have bred terrier genes into many other stocks to produce specialized breeds such as bulldogs. Both the largest terriers (Airedales) and the smallest (Yorkshire terriers) hail from England; Scotland, Wales, and Ireland have each produced numerous terriers as well.

The pharaoh hound, an ancient Egyptian breed whose portrait (*inset*) shows it to have remained unchanged since at least 2000 B.C., when this drawing was placed in a tomb at Beni Hasan, Egypt. The short-haired pharaoh hounds are both runners and ratters, and probably lie close to the ancestry of the terrier group.

The Airedale, hailing from Yorkshire, weighs up to 20 kilograms, just nudging the lower limit of wolf-size. Light as he is, the Airedale is disproportionately dedicated to the hunt and has even been used to capture lions and bears. He is also a good shepherd dog, protecting his flocks from any and all predators, and will even cheerfully function as a retriever. Bold and aggressive, he is nonetheless a working dog of even disposition and great loyalty, a good friend and protector to the family. Moreover, the worthy character of the Airedale is shared by terriers ranging in size all the way down to the tiny Yorkie.

Most terriers seem to have been developed in response to the special requirements of northwestern European agriculture. With the advance of planting and pastoral cultures into the region, a need arose to control those smaller mammals which offered competition to the new farming communities. Such animals—notably foxes, members of the weasel family, and, later, rats of various sorts unintentionally imported from the Near East—exacted as tribute from farmers a significant quantity of crops and small domesticated animals. The original domestic mousers, polecat-ferrets derived from indigenous weasels, lacked the intelligence necessary for free movement within human societies; these were later largely (but not completely) replaced by domesticated cats originating in northern Africa and imported to Europe by the Romans. Such cats, while invaluable inhabitants of granaries, tend only to kill what they require as food, while the rodents attached to farming communities are more than able to compensate by rapid breeding for losses to housecat kills. Thus a new animal, one that would kill more than it required as food, became necessary. In response, the smaller terriers were born of careful selection of prototerrier midgets. But terriers are born not merely to kill; they must also love the chase and, as their name implies, must run their prey to earth. And so the fox terriers, one of the oldest races, were developed. These medium-sized terriers think nothing of entering a fox's den and pulling poor Reynard and his entire family to the surface.

The noble Airedale, a hunter and largest of the true terriers.

A terrier sampler. *From left:* smooth and wirehaired fox terriers; a miniature schnauzer; a Bedlington, whose lamblike appearance is enhanced by clipping its blue-white coat; and a Staffordshire dogfighter.

The tinier breeds were originally used in conjunction with domestic ferrets to kill rabbits and rodents. Ferrets were released into the rodent holes, where their long, supple bodies permitted them easy movement, and their questing drove the inhabitants of these burrows to the surface. Here, little terriers waited to dispatch their prey as it surfaced and before it could flee to other holes. Thus was born the sport of ratting, in which dogs competed for superiority in the number of rats slain at the moment of surfacing. A good ratting terrier may kill hundreds of rodents in a day if the conditions are right, and within the artificial ratting pit a terrier will joyously destroy as many as are offered him. (The record is held by the bullterrier bitch Jenny Lind, who in one and a half hours killed five hundred rats!) Joy, indeed, seems a central aspect of the terrier personality, and these clownish animals are thus valued highly by people desiring companions rather than workers. Their wiry builds, quick (rather more goatlike than doglike) movements, and evident delight with the world have endeared terriers to people all over the world, and new terrier breeds arise wherever dog breeders establish themselves.

As a gruesome footnote to terrier history, when during medieval times the public amusement switched from the notorious "games" of the Roman circus to the cheaper but similarly cruel pastimes of animal-fighting and -baiting,

terrier aggressiveness and tenacity assumed new proportions as entrepreneurs of the dogpits bred new forms for the artificial violence craved by the buying public. Survivors of those horrible times are the bulldogs and bullterriers, originally produced for the management of cattle at the knacker's and later for the bloodthirsty sport of bullbaiting. Several such dogs would be set upon a bull in a ring or in the street of a medieval town, where refreshments would be sold and music played in much the same manner as they are today in the cinema of violence which has largely replaced such sanguinary sport. Small size and powerful jaws permitted these dogs to grab and cling to cattle in spite of being tossed about by their mighty bovine victims. My own parents bred English bulldogs in my youth, and these animals always delighted in gripping a length of rubber hose while being swung around and around in the air by my father. Tiring, he would let go the hose in midarc, sending hose and bulldog careening across the lawn, only to have the dog bound eagerly back to him with that hose for more bullfighting.

While the blood sports of yesterday are largely replaced by television and movies today, dogfight entrepreneurs continue to practice their "sport" throughout the world. In this context the various pit bullterriers, brand-new (less than a century old) breeds designed especially for the destruction of their own kind, have appeared on both sides of the Atlantic and even in Australia. Americans, especially, seem interested in the organized dogfight; pit bulls, while not recognized as showbreeds by most kennel clubs, are already a distinctive race in the United States. Wiry and boxerlike in face, these midgets (weighing about 10 kilograms) are, oddly enough, among the kindest of dogs until *taught* their work in the pit. Puppies are encouraged to kill rats, kittens, and

Specialized cattle-herding and fighting dogs of terrier origin include (*from left*) the bullterrier, boxer, and bulldog. All are selected for strength of bite, a character reflected in the comparatively large size of their heads.

---

other small mammals to bring out the proper bloodthirstiness, for pit bulls raised in the home show no more than the usual terrier aggressiveness toward other dogs. With their mighty jaws, superb musculature, and never-say-die attitude, pit bulls offer fights to the death. Such battling is, of course, unusual in the canid world, where fighting is carefully regulated by inborn systems of ritual appeasement to avoid severe injury. It required centuries of careful artificial breeding, coupled with intensive teaching of puppies, to eliminate these protective rituals in the origination of the fighting breeds. Like nuclear weapons, pit bullterriers and the dogfight bring into broad question the applicability of our species name, "Man the Wise."

As mentioned at the beginning of the chapter, midget dogs represent only one of two routes by which small dogs may be developed. The other may be called dwarfing, and is characterized by small size resulting from a mutation producing the condition known as achondroplasia, in which the cartilage of the bone-ends grows improperly. In human beings, achondroplasia occurs about once in 10,000 births; from time immemorial, such dwarves have been valued as court jesters, clerks, and other specialized functionaries, for the condition in no way affects intelligence or health. As a matter of fact, achondroplastic dwarves often show greater than ordinary physical vitality, and the ancient Egyptians left whole graveyards whose only inhabitants were dwarves bred by their pharaonic masters.

Signs of achondroplasia appear during fetal development of skeletal structure. Cartilage, the gristly tissue that in later life normally metamorphoses into bone, develops its bony character much earlier in achondroplastic dwarves. This anomaly results in curved, stunted limbs and the early cessation of growth of the facial bones, producing the characteristic pug-nosed, large-headed aspect of both human and canine dwarves. Stubby paws, with short toes and large joints, are also typical of the mutation in dogs, as are backward-tilted hipbones that sometimes interfere with the birthing of young by dwarf females. In the wild, of course, such stunted creatures would not survive, but under human care an astonishing panoply of dwarf breeds has arisen to trouble this author and others more accustomed to the graceful, long-limbed structure appropriate to canids.

Perhaps most ancient of the achondroplastic breeds is the Pekingese of China, dating back at least 3,000 years. Likely bred from chow ancestry, Pekingese dogs are long-haired—so much so that their twisted little legs are completely concealed beneath a skirt of hair more appropriate in length to their big chow ancestors. Called "little lion-dogs" or "butterfly-lions" by their Oriental breeders, Pekingese were highly prized by their aristocratic masters in the courts of China. The theft of such a little brute could result in a

Rendering of the skull of a Pekingese achondroplastic dwarf dog superimposed on the outline of the skull of the wolf ancestor. Note the extreme compression of the Peke's facial region, a character typical of achondroplasia; this skull is so altered that the teeth are barely rooted in the maxillary bone, and the dog must eat artificially "pre-chewed" food or die.

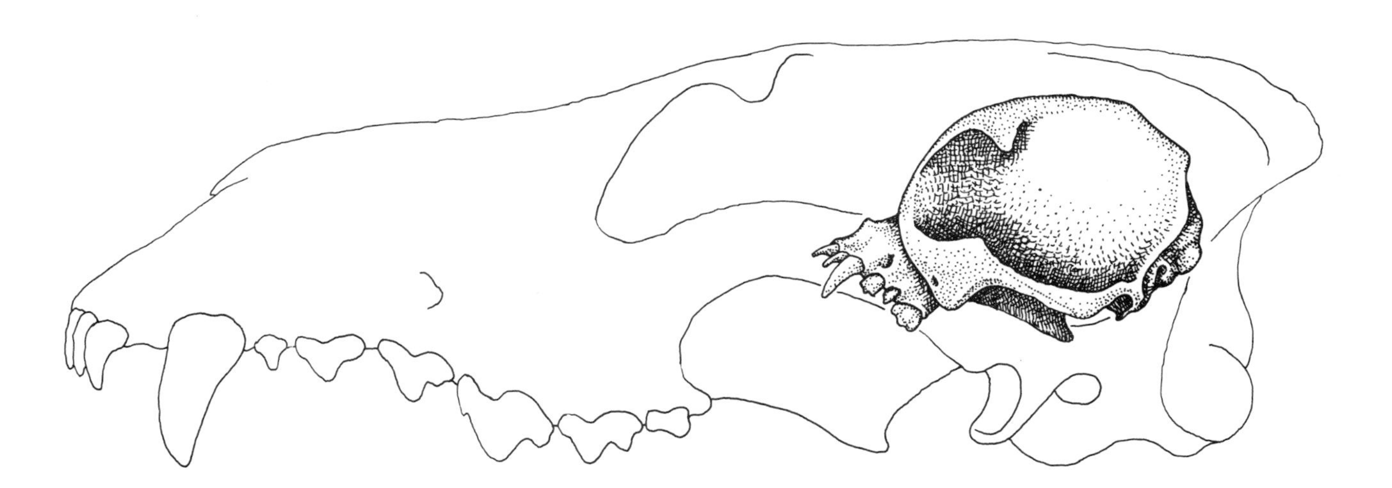

A human and two canine (Pekingese) achondroplastic dwarves. In both man and dog, achondroplasia results in compression of the face, shortening and thickening of the limbs, and backward curvature of the hips. The inset shows an achondroplastic human dwarf's skull superimposed over that of a normal man.

---

slow and horrible death for the thief. A few Pekingese were stolen by British agents and exported to England in 1860, where they enjoyed immediate popularity. Now they are everywhere valued possessions of city dwellers, for these little (2 to 3 kilograms) animals are totally dependent on human beings and uniquely suited to conditions of confinement.

Indeed, so dwarfed and twisted are Pekingese that they are unable even to eat as other dogs do; their teeth are incompletely rooted in their miserably stunted jaws, so that their diets must consist of specially prepared soft foods. The Chinese are said to have used slave girls to nurse these dwarves, first killing the rightful offspring of the slaves. Thus the origin of the Pekingese is not only a reflection of human inhumanity to the canid stock, but of human inhumanity to human beings themselves. Small wonder that I scamper to the other side of the street when I see such a dog approaching.

Orientals also bred the Shih Tzu ("Son of Lion"), perhaps as long ago as they did the Pekingese; the first literary reference to the breed appeared in A.D. 624. Like the Pekingese, the Shih Tzu is a totally man-dependent breed with a coat as impractical as its build. Another Oriental is the "English" toy spaniel, which is really of Chinese or Japanese origin and dates perhaps from 2500 B.P. The Chinese also produced the pug, introduced to Europe by traders of the Dutch East India Company in the seventeenth century. A short-haired breed, the pug may represent an admixture of the dominant achondroplastic genes in some early mastiff stock, for a mastiff and a pug placed side by side present astounding caricatures of each other in coat texture, coloring, and even facial expression.

One wonders, in retrospect, whether the Orientals isolated all of the achondroplastic genes now present in so many breeds. Certainly, a host of new crosses—"Peke-a-poos" (Pekingese × toy poodle) and the like—are

A pug, probably originating as a sort of "dwarf giant" of mastiff stock.

A dwarf sampler, showing achondroplastic characteristics superimposed on the genetic structures of diverse types of dogs. *Above*: the Pembrokeshire corgi is a dwarf cattledog of polar type; the Scottie is a dwarf terrier. *Below*: the basset hound is a sort of "dwarfed giant" of acromegalic bloodhound ancestry, a kind of "canine tank" for rapid movement through heavy brush; the Boston bullterrier is a midget terrier with typical achondroplasia of the face.

springing up around the world from Oriental stock. Still, achondroplasia has long been apparent in many old Western breeds; among polar breeds the corgis (from the Welsh *cor*, "dwarf," and *gi*, "dog"), cattledogs of the British Isles, exhibit strongly achondroplastic legs that permit them to dash easily and safely between the legs of their giant wards. Dachshunds, basset hounds, cocker spaniels (and their novel and terrible offspring, the "cock-a-poo" cross between these short-legged spaniels and toy poodles), Scottish and other short-legged terriers reflect achondroplastic admixture. Bulldogs possess faces of achondroplastic type superimposed on a mastiff background, so that the short jaws of these breeds are possessed of immense strength due to muscles operating from a mastiff-sized cranium. The bowlegged appearance of English bulldogs is another reflection of this racial mixing. In all, almost any dog departing markedly in skeletal form from the old canid framework may be suspected of hiding an achondroplastic dwarf in its ancestral woodpile.

CANIDS IN THE WORLD OF MAN

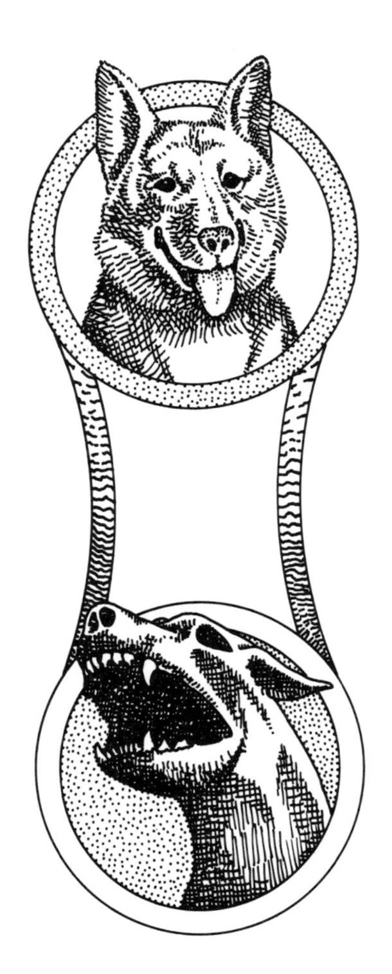

Opening this chapter are portraits of two famous dogs from the literature of modern times: above, Rin Tin Tin, archetype of the shepherd dog, intelligent, loyal, ever concerned with the well-being of his masters; below, Sir Arthur Conan Doyle's Hound of the Baskervilles, archetype of the darker dog-place that lurks within us all. The Hound's lunatic howling was superbly dredged by Conan Doyle from the ancient wolf-time, arousing in the reader a horror of the long ages during which people shared their ranges and fare with wolves, the king canids. Now, along with so many other wild canids, the wolf is on the way out. Still, as these drawings suggest, he lives on in our dogs—the dog's loyalty to his group, his sagacity, and his potential for evil are all derived from his wolfish ancestry. More broadly, the dog is our last intimate look at the wild in the form of another mammalian mind, and both sides of the canid coin are very much apparent in him.

North Americans and others of European descent tend in modern times to regard dogs as pets—companions, friends, loving slaves. This is an unusual relationship, however, one born of the plenty to which Europeans and North Americans are accustomed. In most other times and places, such plenty has been nonexistent and the position of the dog far more utilitarian, to say the least. In those societies—the Eskimo, for instance—where the dog's function is more reflective of the original situation, the pooch remains a strictly utilitarian tool, providing motive power for sledges. He is also occasionally an item of food when times get hard, and if lucky, he gets to participate in the hunt. The Eskimo is not kind to dogs, and the Eskimo dog is not ordinarily affectionate to his master. Both are reflections of the hard life at the edge of the world, wherein there is little room for the companionable sort of man-dog relationship with which readers of this book are probably familiar.

Once dogs assumed shepherd status, watching over semidomesticated flocks of sheep, goats, or cattle, they became somewhat closer to their human masters—at least with regard to interspecific communication between man and dog. Still, working shepherd dogs remain with the sheep, as do sheepdogs, and are not "pets" in the conventional sense. The rise of giant dogs used as guards and in war brought the symbiosis still closer; as housedogs and companions-in-arms, canids proved indispensable at an early date. Even today, however, working guard dogs remain somewhat aloof from all but their handlers; they must, for their duty is to oppose, not to befriend.

Indeed, many a breed had its origin as an attacker of human beings. The Rhodesian Ridgeback, descended from a cross between bloodhounds (themselves designed as trackers of men) and native African pariah-dingo hunting dogs, was in the beginning a patroller of the boundaries of colonial African plantations. Much touted today as a "lion hunter," the Ridgeback more probably began his work as a deterrent to native Africans' prowling the European settlements; certainly a pack of these big, protective dogs is unhealthy for a stranger to trifle with.

The ridge of permanently erected hair along the back of a Rhodesian Ridgeback presents an attitude of aggressiveness even when the dog is playing. A stranger, reading this apparent signal, is thus rendered very careful in the dog's presence.

The Doberman pinscher is another case in point. This century-old breed originated as the lifework of one Ludwig Dobermann of Apolda, Germany, who desired to produce a perfect police and guard dog. Derived in part from local cattledogs and black-and-tan Manchester terriers, the Doberman is still classed by some authorities as a terrier—making this big (up to 35 kilograms) breed by far the largest of the terrier lot. Dobermans are famed for their nervous temperaments and highly territorial natures, ideal characteristics in dogs designed to fight human beings. A further refinement of the Doberman ability to handle unruly men is the practice of cropping the lop-ears and docking the long tails of Doberman pups in order that a man may be afforded less chance to protect himself by gripping one of these appendages.

These silhouettes of Doberman pinschers before (*left*) and after cropping and docking illustrate the potential for postnatal manipulation of the form of dogs. The cropped, erect ears of an American Doberman (the British do not ordinarily mutilate the breed) present an aspect of aggressiveness even when the dog is at rest, while the docked tail helps conceal any friendliness that might be betrayed by wagging.

Modern dogs have also been forced to invade a new niche as laboratory animals. Here, kept in rows of kennel runs, they smoke cigarettes, drink alcohol, and otherwise model the common human vices—and die in the service of science. Unlike other common laboratory animals, dogs have good, strong canid voices; certain laboratory manuals recommend the cutting of laboratory dogs' vocal cords, so that the miserable beasts will suffer in silence. It is interesting to speculate about the degree to which the emotions of experimenters must be dulled to permit their committing such acts repeatedly.

We have touched on certain breeds that originated primarily as sources of food. Today, the breeders of such dogs (notably chows) are pleased to ignore this somber element in their pets' past, preferring to regard them as, say, hunters or guard dogs. Nonetheless, many—most, perhaps—societies around the world regard a good dog as a good meal, European prejudices notwithstanding. Those of my acquaintance who have tried it say that dog tastes very much like lamb, my own favorite domestic red meat. While I have not yet breached my ancient Anglo prejudice against munching mutts, I have read many recipes for dog which would sound extremely appetizing if the meat were lamb instead.

With regard to the eating of dogs by human beings, it is interesting to note that there are very few dogs (or cats) remaining in China. The teeming population of that enlightened land, in response to the dicta of the Maoist revolution, appears to have eaten most of them within the past thirty or so years to rid the country of possible competitors for food. For centuries, China has had the best and most varied recipes for dog, still regarded as a delicacy there. I read recently of the noble response of a Szechuan People's Commissariat to the plea of an elite restaurant catering to foreign visitors: Dogs were unavailable! What to do? The Commissariat immediately detailed a number of peasants to search the neighborhood for dogs, with the happy result that enough were found to entertain a number of visiting dignitaries with the very best Szechuan Thousand Happiness Pooch Pie (or whatever). Only a Socialist Workers' Paradise could function so smoothly.

In other parts of the world, there have been times when, possessing naught but dog's flesh and man's flesh for food, human beings have preferred eating their own kind. Among peoples as diverse as the Polynesians of the Pacific and the Fuegians of the southern tip of South America, the tale is similar; the choice is not, perhaps, one of taste, but rather one of expedience. As one Fuegian put it, on being questioned by Europeans about his people's eating their women but sparing their dogs during hard times: "Dog catch otter. Woman no catch otter." Similarly, the Maori and other Pacific seafaring folk relied on their pariah-dingo dogs to test new lands for hostile inhabitants. Stuck at sea for months at a time, they sometimes fell to eating one another, but they always saved dogs for the crucial test of landfall.

Which does little good for dogs in the modern world. Recalling, as we must, the present nutritional status of the planet's 5,000,000,000 human beings, almost 4,000,000,000 of whom cannot get enough protein for optimum physical development, we come to the appalling situation in the United States, where some 10,000,000 dogs are killed each year by humane societies and other animal control units. It is estimated by the Humane Society of the United States that some 50,000,000 to 80,000,000 dogs inhabit the nation at present, with perhaps 2,000 pups being born *each hour*. Estimating an average of 4 kilograms per dog killed in vacuum chambers and by injection of sodium Pentothal, and multiplying this conservative average by 10,000,000, we come to 40,000 *metric tons* of dog flesh consigned annually to crematoria and "sanitary landfills" across the United States. China, eat your heart out.

Yet our peculiar image of dogs-as-people prevents our making any productive use of the immense tonnage of protein we waste yearly in the slaying of stray dogs. Indeed, many humane societies and pounds that kill large numbers of dogs are unwilling to pass even the inert bodies of these unwanted canids to such interested parties as schools wishing to perform dissections. In this respect we resemble the Europe of medieval times, when the dissection of human cadavers was forbidden by ecclesiastical and secular law. Certainly, the suggestion that dog protein be passed on to persons willing to eat it would raise the hackles of any self-righteous proprietor of a pound—to whom such an idea might well smack of cannibalism.

Dogs that do not have the good fortune to share in the food supply of a human household but that manage to evade the dogcatcher's net are in for a worse time in the twilight econiche occupied by feral (domestic-gone-wild) carnivores. In cities, their lives tend to be "nasty, brutish, and short," for the city as we know it will not support the reproduction of feral animals larger than cats; competition for food from rats, cats, and birds is too intense, and the more conspicuous dogs are always easy prey for the ever-present dogcatcher. In warmer rural areas, on the other hand, feral dogs often do quite well. Here, lacking the fear of man that governs much of the behavior of their wild canid cousins, such dogs often become killers of livestock and wild game in the manner of their wolfish ancestors. Because the common belief is that "nice doggies would never do such things," the blame for these killings is often shifted to such wild canids as coyotes, which suffer intensified persecution as a result.

Although it is easy for dogs to enter a feral state, they do not generally produce breeding feral populations except in regions free of harsh winters, due to the artificially induced breeding cycle of *Canis familiaris*. Unlike all wild canids, whose periods of estrus and whelping are precisely keyed by rigorous natural selection to the seasons of the year, domestic dogs may enjoy two or more breeding periods a year, these occurring quite independent of local climatic peculiarities. Thus, clans of feral dogs tend to attenuate in numbers over the years, or to be absorbed into native populations of wild canids such as wolves and coyotes.

The domestic dog is possessed of something of a split personality; the docile sheepdog herding his flock by day may turn into a vicious sheep-slayer by night, and suburban pets allowed to run in groups quickly assume the pack-hunting character of their ancestors, often killing (but not eating—they eat at home) livestock and even other dogs. Almost any domestic dog will feel a surge of desire at the sight of a running deer, and wherever deer persist in large numbers, pet dogs are a nuisance. Because human beings like to kill deer themselves, they take great exception to any dog's doing it first. Still, many rural folk cannot believe that their kindly housedog would even *think* of bothering Bambi—but refuse, at the same time, to tie up old Strongheart at night.

And now we come to a strange place in the relationship between man and dog: a place of fear—that place from which springs the Hound of the Baskervilles. There have been (and will be again) many intervals during which the dogs of a people have turned against them, and have slain men and women and little children and cracked human bones in the setting of the sun. When the social fabric rots and tears away, when contracts between men are ignored and reason fails at last, and especially when the food supply is interrupted, both human beings and their canid symbiotes take to the streets to finish the job begun by social entropy. We are reminded of a Pompeiian room isolated by the mud of Vesuvius, in which were found two skeletons, one of a woman and one of a dog. That of the dog remained perfectly articulated, but the woman's bones were scattered about the room, their ends gnawed by the dog that had, for a time, survived her.

A famous plaster cast taken of the space left in Pompeiian volcanic muds by a dog's decaying body.

Starvation, as the Fuegian illustrated, has a way of overcoming even the most elementary scruples in dogs as well as humans. In this time of increasing scarcity, with prices rising even higher as greater numbers of people scramble for diminishing food resources, we Americans with our 80,000,000 dogs may soon begin thinking more of the Chinese and of that Pompeiian dog. In the radioactive slagland that our politicians offer us as a future, it may be that the fast-evolving, ever-adaptable canids, the dogs of our own making, will share the apex of creation with insects and rats.

The potential for their survival (if we don't eat them first) is definitely there; as we have seen, there are at least 200 distinct breeds of domestic dogs, the American Kennel Club alone recognizing 123. Here, of course, we haven't had nearly enough room to treat each of these breeds. Instead, we have been examining domestic dogs as a biological species, a unique branch of the great canid family tree. More than this, however, domestic dogs are an example of the capacity of natural variation, under purposeful guidance, to produce radically new forms in a comparatively short time. This capacity has some interesting implications, not only for breeders of dogs but also for the lunatic potential of politicians everywhere. Canids and human beings are on a genetic and physiological par with one another, equally highly evolved in all respects except brain development, and both species exhibit a similarly broad capacity for variation. Throughout history, many politicians have dreamed of creating races of supermen, born-docile workers, or other hereditary castes of human beings (giant Roman gladiators and dwarf Egyptian clerics being two historic examples). The ease with which the form and temperament of dogs have been molded by genetic selection cannot but excite the imagination of would-be perfecters of humanity.

We are reminded of the *magnum opus* of J. R. R. Tolkien, the *Lord of the Rings* trilogy, in which assorted breeds of hominids (he doesn't call them "men") race to and fro across a somber landscape called Middle-Earth. Although this great tale is customarily assigned to some imaginary point in the remote past, we are led to believe that many, if not all, of the peoples involved are products of artificial breeding: Orcs, for instance, are the born soldiers of Tolkien's world, sporting the dim-witted noncommissioned truculence appropriate to good infantry. Dwarves are "tough, thrawn . . . secretive, laborious, lovers of stone, of gems, of things that take shape under the hands of the craftsman rather than of things that live by their own life." Perfectly bred miners, in short; free of the labor unrest that characterizes the imperfectly adapted miners of our own time. Such sophisticated manipulation of human genetics argues well for the saga's relocation into the distant future, a post-technological Hell of warring man-breeds.

As with Tolkien's hominids, so with our own canids; they fit their man-made econiches precisely. Breeds used in specialized forms of hunting, for instance, often converge in form with their prey. Take the greyhound and the dachshund. Although both descend from a common ancestry, the greyhound reflects in form the antelope for whose pursuit it was designed, much as the short-legged dachshund parallels its badger prey. In temperament, the grey-

Rendering of fictional examples of extreme artificial breeding of human beings. In *Lord of the Rings*, the Orc (*left*) is one of the infantry of bad guys; the Dwarf (*right*) is a miner, small, stout, a lover of the dark. The conception of such characters parallels our creation of specialized breeds of dogs.

Physical parallels between canine hunters and their prey. *Above:* a greyhound and a gazelle; *below:* the doughty badger and his equally doughty dachshund adversary.

hound is skittish like the antelope, the dachshund doughty and tenacious like the badger. Convergence in function is carried to extremes in those "toy" breeds designed to replace children in the affections of their masters: the Pekingese, with its infantile dependence on premasticated food and protection by its effete owner, closely parallels the helpless human infant. For a person wanting a sense of mission in the world, the care of such a congenitally crippled creature as a Pekingese can provide all manner of solace.

Whatever specialized role he may play, the dog always offers friendship for the taking. For me, the big pointy-eared mutts I love offer this and more; in their unruliness, in their sensitivity and swiftness and predatory manners, they epitomize the vanishing world of the wild Canidae from which they descend.

We mentioned back in the chapter on domestication that each domestic breed of dog represents an isolated subset of wolf genes sieved from the whole by human intervention. Through the centuries the breeds have become ever more genetically isolated from one another as their human sponsors' striving for "perfection"—especially with regard to showdogs—resulted in progressive inbreeding. Unless the breeder cages his aristocratic wards within high fences, however, there is always the possibility that some unspeakable cur will sow a few wild oats among the carefully isolated purebred gene pool.

Then what have you? You have a mutt, of course, a mongrel, a member of the most variegated and widespread of "breeds," that "breed" most despised by persons concerned more with pedigree and appearance than with adaptability. Working backward in time, we can metaphorically call the wolf a sort of "ultimate mutt," in that the modern dog breeds are essentially distillations via selective inbreeding of certain aspects of wolfishness. Indeed, in places where mutts of various descents interbreed uninhibitedly (as mutts always do), their progeny tend more and more to resemble in form and coloration the wolves from which they all ultimately descend.

Behavorial characteristics as well as physical form enter into breeders' motives for establishing and maintaining isolated strains of dogs; these, too, blend again in mutts to recreate to some extent the generalized genius of the wolf—albeit largely minus the traits, such as ritualized nose biting, that were so long ago eliminated from domestic dogs. In short, the more "muttly" a dog becomes as a result of successive crossbreedings, the more adaptable he seems.

As an example, I know of certain fox terriers who will not tolerate cats, whether or not the terriers and cats are raised in one another's company. Fox terriers were originally constructed to prey on creatures of cat-size, and this genetic imperative often supersedes any amount of training to the otherwise. On the other hand, my own mutt, Rufus, who could easily bisect any cat with a snap of his long jaws, takes great delight in kittens, allowing the little devils to clamber over his face, leap at his feet from concealment, and otherwise act in a manner that to a fox terrier might be insulting to a capital degree. Still, raised in other circumstances, Rufus would no doubt kill cats with the same enthusiasm that he shows in dispatching jackrabbits (nice cat-sized prey that these big hares are).

In short, the mutt is by definition more of a generalist than are most "purebred" dogs, and his behavior is therefore more a result of environmental conditions—teaching, the attitudes of his owners, and so on—than is that of a dog bred for heritable behavorial traits. With all this in mind, it seems a pity that so many otherwise well-informed folk are unwilling to take on a dog of "questionable," or mixed, background. For anyone wishing an intelligent, adaptable companion in a dog, mutts are almost invariably superior to the nervous, inbred, pedigreed creatures created for specific attributes of appearance and behavior.

But, alas, too many people acquire dogs simply as statements of their own personal social status (or some status they wish attributed to them). Then, stuck with a high-strung, unbiddable setter, an aggressive Doberman pinscher, or a sickly Pekingese, such people find themselves unable to adjust happily to their inbred wards and attribute to dogdom in general the idiosyncrasies of their own specimens.

In discussing mutts, I would be remiss if I neglected the "purest-bred" mutt of all, the lurcher of the British Isles. The verb *lurch* (or *lurk*) originally meant "to poach game"; in medieval England, a lurcher was one who survived by hunting illegally in the forests and parklands of the aristocracy and the Church. The poachers of Merrie England were of course at the lower end of the social spectrum and therefore were forced to utilize the cheapest of canine allies in their forbidden hunting. Almost any dog would do in these pursuits, but those showing a good aptitude for stealth (the punishments for lurchers, both human and canine, were indeed terrible) were favored over noisier specimens. Also, medium to large size was necessary in the pursuit and tackling of deer and boar, while a good sense of communication between man and dog—silent, inconspicuous communication via hand signals, whispering, and even facial expression—was of the essence in lands bristling with milord's bloodthirsty game wardens.

In short, the human lurcher required a canine counterpart who was smart, perceptive, quiet, powerful, and swift. Through the centuries, poachers selected from among strays and cheap pups those dogs exhibiting just such qualities, producing in the end mutts whose name—"lurchers"—amply reflects their origins and, by implication, their personal attributes.

Today, there are efforts under way to recreate the lurcher; indeed, to establish a true *breed* of that name. Such efforts must founder, however, for "lurching" is more an activity than a breed name. Lurchers are variously portrayed in old paintings as resembling shaggy German shepherd dogs, whippet-terrier crosses, houndly sheepdogs, and any number of gradations between these types. In some parts of modern England a lurcher is simply a mutt—no more, no less; my own Rufus, in fact, would make a great lurcher. Perhaps those of us who advocate the ownership of mutts might adopt this fine old name for them, with its connotations of sagacity and partnership-in-adversity with human beings. It was these attributes that produced domestic dogs, and for most of us the same attributes remain all-important in our choice of canine companions. To the New Lurcher, then, the mutt in all his variety, I would (if I could) grant the crown of dogdom.

In tracing the annals of the Canidae through their millions of years, I hope I have communicated some of the magic of the family. It *is* magic, too; magic born of aeons of selection among both canids and hominids for intelligence and adaptability, and culminating in this wonderful, multifaceted symbiosis between human beings and dogs. And the other canids, the wolves and wild dogs and foxes of the world, all abundantly share the magnificent character of our own dogs. There remains a measure of hope that our respect for these delightful creatures will save them from our peculiarly human rapacity. Unfortunately, the old stereotypes—the ferocity of the wolf, the cunning of the fox, the cowardliness of the jackal—are all more accurately applied to human beings of the sort most opposed to these animals. Giving intelligence and adaptability their honest evolutionary due, we might begin to cherish the undomesticated branches of the family Canidae and the wild world of which they are part. Such cherishing would indeed be a positive measure of our own intelligence and adaptability, as well as an indication that we're able to muster as much love and loyalty for our planetary landscape as do our dogs for us.

APPENDIX: LIVING CANID GENERA AND SPECIES

Vulpes, foxes, eleven species
bengalensis, Bengali fox
canus, southwest Asian or Blanford's fox
chama, Cape silver fox
cinereoargentatus, gray fox
corsac, corsac fox
ferrilatus, Tibetan sand fox
leucopus, Indian desert fox
pallida, pale fox
rüppelli, sand fox
velox, swift or kit fox
vulpes, red fox
Dusicyon, South American canids, eight species, most called "foxes"
culpaeolus, zorro
culpaeus, culpeo fox
fulvipes, zorro
griseus, pampas fox
gymnocercus, zorro
inca, Inca fox
sechurae, zorro
vetulus, zorro
Alopex lagopus, Arctic fox
Atelocynus microtus, zorro
Cerdocyon thous, crab-eating fox (sometimes included in genus *Dusicyon—D. cancrivorus*)

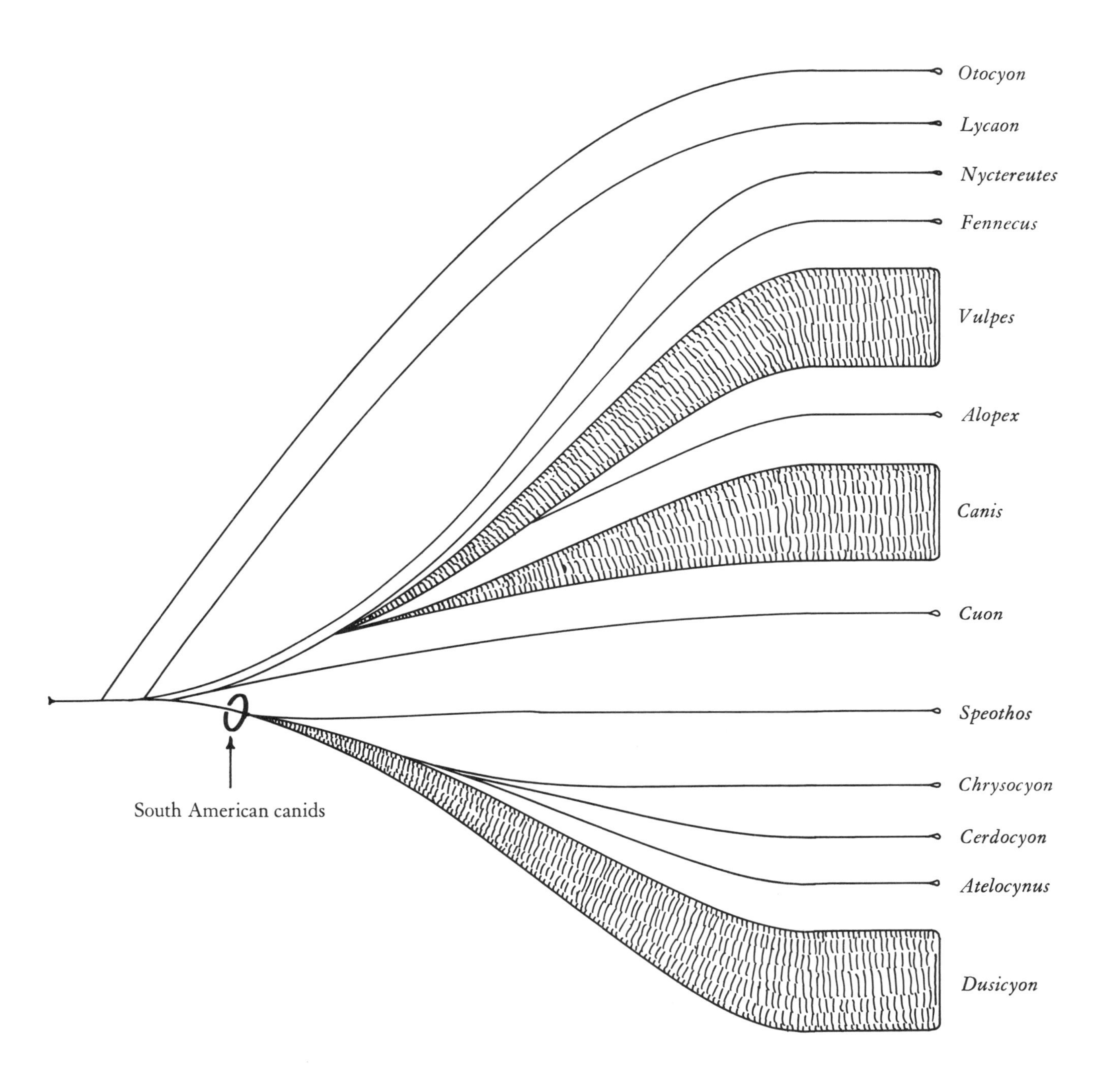

The adaptive radiation of modern canids from a *Tomarctus*-like ancestor.

Chrysocyon brachyurus, maned wolf
Cuon alpinus, dhole
Fennecus zerda, fennec
Lycaon pictus, Cape hunting dog
Nyctereutes procyonoides, raccoon dog
Otocyon megalotis, bat-eared fox
Speothos venaticus, bush dog (this and the three single-species genera *A. microtus*, *C. thous*, and *C. brachyurus*, along with *Dusicyon*, are all South American)
Canis, dogs, nine species
adustus, side-striped jackal
aureus, golden jackal
dingo, dingo
familiaris, domestic dog
latrans, coyote
lupus, wolf
mesomelas, black-backed jackal
niger, red wolf
simensis, Simenian jackal

GLOSSARY

achondroplasia A congenital anomaly of the skeleton characterized by early cessation of bone growth and resulting in a form of dwarfism.

acromegaly A congenital anomaly of the pituitary gland characterized by continuation of bone growth well into adulthood and resulting in enlargement of the extremities and a form of gigantism.

adaptive radiation The invasion by a newly successful organism of a number of econiches unavailable to its ancestors. This eventually produces the division of a single species into many species adapted to specialized life-styles; the process of division is a "radiation."

Aeluroidea The superfamily of catlike carnivores including families Viverridae, Hyaenidae, and Felidae.

Amphicyon "Part-dog," an extinct genus of primitive bearlike canids.

Anubis The ancient Egyptian jackal-god, conductor of the dead to the Otherworld.

Arctocyonidae "Bear-dogs," an extinct condylarth family of primitive carnivorous mammals; they were, in truth, neither bears nor dogs. See *Condylarthra.*

articular quadrate A form of jaw-joint typical of reptiles, in which a small articular bone at the rear of the lower jaw hinges against a movable quadrate bone in the skull.

biomass The sum total of living matter in an ecosystem.

Borhyaenidae An extinct family of carnivorous South American marsupials.

canid Of or pertaining to the family Canidae.

Canidae The family of dogs and foxes.

canine Of or pertaining to dogs; also, the "dog-tooth," the long stabbing tooth to the rear of the incisors characteristic of dogs, most other mammals, and synapsids.

Canis The genus of true dogs, wolves, and jackals.

canoid Of or pertaining to superfamily Canoidea.

Canoidea The superfamily of doglike carnivores including families Mustelidae, Procyonidae, Ursidae, and Canidae.

carnassial Any of a pair of specialized flesh-shearing teeth located on each side of the mouth in flesh-eating mammals.

Carnivora The order of higher flesh-eating mammals.

carnivory A way of life oriented around flesh eating.

caudal gland A gland located on the base of the tail of canids which offers pheromonal information concerning an individual's sexual status.

Condylarthra An extinct order of flesh-eating mammals more closely related to modern hoofed forms than to the true Carnivora.

Creodonta An extinct suborder of Carnivora with primitive carnassial tooth arrangements.

cropping The custom of trimming the ears of some breeds of dogs, most commonly terriers and their kin.

dentary-squamosal A form of jaw-joint typical of mammals, in which the massive dentary comprising the lower jaw is hinged to a squamosal bone embedded solidly in the skull. The old reptilian articular-quadrate joint is, in mammals, reduced to a pair of tiny bones inside the ear.

digitigrade Walking on the toes so as to lengthen the effective stride.

dingo The aboriginal wild dog of Australia, brought to that continent by early men.

dinosaur Any of the advanced terrestrial vertebrates that dominated Earth's continental ecosystems during the Mesozoic Era, between about 230,000,000 and 65,000,000 years ago.

docking — The custom of amputating the tails of certain breeds of dogs.

dromaeosaur — Any of a family of swift, two-legged, man-sized dinosaurs which probably hunted large prey in social units.

Dusicyon — A genus of eight species of South American canids of generally foxlike appearance and habits.

dwarf — Any unusually small and oddly proportioned animal.

ectothermy — "Heating-from-without," a form of body-temperature regulation dependent on the collecting of heat directly from external sources, as in reptiles.

endothermy — "Heating-from-within," a form of body-temperature regulation based on the metabolic release of heat from food and largely independent of outside temperature, as in mammals.

Felidae — The family of cats.

Fissipeda — The land-dwelling suborder of order Carnivora—i.e., those with "split feet," or separate toes.

Flehmen — The lip-curling motion of a dog that is sampling scent with the Jacobson's organs located in the roof of its mouth.

fox — Any of the smaller wild canids.

herbivory — Specialization for a plant-eating way of life.

Hesperocyon — "Western Dog," an extinct genus of small catlike canids of western North America.

hominid — A member of the family Hominidae of manlike bipedal primates.

hound, gaze- — An ancient group of swift domestic hunting dogs that follow prey primarily by sight and are typified by the greyhound.

hound, scent- — An ancient group of partly acromegalic domestic hunting dogs that locate prey primarily by scent and are typified by the bloodhound.

Hyaenidae — The family of hyenas, most social of the Aeluroidea (q.v.).

Hyaenodontidae — A family of creodont carnivores whose carnassial teeth were upper second molars shearing against lower third molars; they became extinct around 12,000,000 years ago. See *Creodonta*.

incisor Any of the cutting foreteeth in mammals.

insectivore An insect-eater; more specifically, a member of the order Insectivora of primitive placental mammals.

lop-ear A congenital condition in many domestic dogs, in which the pinna of the adult hangs loosely at the side of the head rather than standing erect, as in wild canids.

marsupial Any of the subclass Metatheria of "pouched" mammals, whose young are born at a far more incomplete and vulnerable level of development than are those of the higher, or placental, mammals.

mastiff Any of the group of giant acromegalic domestic dog breeds.

megalosaur Any of a family of large carnivorous dinosaurs which appear to have hunted their prey in groups.

Mesonychidae "Mid-claws," an extinct family of condylarth flesh-eaters.

Miacidae The founding family of the modern order Carnivora. Miacids were lithe, tree-dwelling, probably squirrel-hunting creatures whose carnassial tooth-pair was upper fourth premolar shearing against lower first molar, as in all living Carnivora.

midget Any unusually small but normally proportioned animal.

molar Any of the rear or grinding teeth in mammals and synapsids.

Mustelidae The family of weasels, skunks, otters, badgers, and their kin, most primitive of canoid mammals.

Neolithic The period of human prehistory approximately postdating the extinction of giant game animals and predating the wholesale rise of agriculture; variously set between perhaps 15,000 and 8,000 years ago.

neopallium The "new cloak," the higher cerebral associative center characteristic of mammalian brains.

neoteny Retention into adulthood of infantile characters.

oestrus The period of "heat" or sexual receptivity, in most mammalian females.

omnivory A way of life based on the ability to eat both animal and vegetable foods.

orbital angle The angle between the horizontal and a line drawn from the top of a canid's skull to the outer edge of its cheekbone; often used to distinguish between the skulls of domestic dogs (whose orbital angle tends to be larger) and those of wild canids.

Orcinus The genus of orcas, or "killer whales," seagoing mammalian social hunters.

Osteoborus The "Bone-crusher," a genus of extinct hyenalike dogs.

Oxyaenidae "Sharp Ones," an extinct family of heavy-skulled creodont carnivores.

panting A physiological reflex for cooling the body, in which water is evaporated from the linings of the breathing passages by increased airflow due to rapid breathing.

pariah dog Any of an ancient complex of domestic or semidomestic North African and southern Asian dogs characterized by short coats and sharply curved sickle-tails.

pheromone An odor used in information exchange between animals.

pinna (pl. *pinnae*) The external sound-collecting earflaps typical of mammals.

Pinnipedia The aquatic suborder ("Fin-feet") or order Carnivora, including seals, walruses, and sea lions.

placental Any of the subclass Eutheria of higher mammals, whose prenatal young are nourished directly from the mother's bloodstream via a specialized organ called the placenta.

plantigrade Walking on the sole of the foot rather than on the toes.

polar dog Any of an ancient complex of domestic dogs of typically wolflike appearance whose ancestor was likely the large northern wolf.

polytypic Having many forms; the domestic dog is a polytypic species.

premolar In mammals, any of the series of shearing teeth lying aft of the canine teeth and forward of the molars.

primate Any of the order Primates of lemurs, tarsioids, monkeys, apes, and men.

Procyonidae The family of doglike carnivores including raccoons and their kin and lying near the base of both the bear family and that of true dogs and foxes.

sheepdog Any dog whose function is to herd sheep.

shepherd dog Any dog whose function is to guard sheep.

sickle-tail A congenital condition in many domestic dogs, in which the tail is carried curved and high rather than straight, as in wild canids.

Simocyon An extinct genus of short-faced dogs that were probably scavengers.

stop The abrupt rise of the forehead characteristic of infant canids and many adult domestic dogs.

symbiosis "Living together," any prolonged and characteristic interaction between two or more dissimilar species; the domestication of the dog by human beings is a form of symbiosis.

synapsid Any of a subclass of Synapsida of extinct reptilelike antecedents of mammals.

terrier A complex of "earth dogs," smallish but powerful domestic hunting dogs designed to kill or at least grapple physically with their prey.

testosterone The male hormone governing much competitive and territorial behavior in mammals.

therapsid Any of the order Therapsida of higher mammallike synapsids.

thylacine The "marsupial wolf," an Australian and Tasmanian flesh-eater of dog-size currently thought extinct as a result of the activity of human beings and true dogs.

Tomarctus "Cutting-bear," an extinct genus of North American canids, the first of essentially modern type. *Tomarctus* lived about 10,000,000 years ago, and seems to have founded the living family Canidae.

toy A tiny dog, especially one with no real function except that of amusing human beings.

Ursidae The family of bears.

Viverridae The most primitive of aeluroid families, that containing mongooses, linsangs, genets, and their kin.

viverrid kill A mode of attack in which a predator seizes its prey by the head or neck and shakes it rapidly; typical of viverrids and all higher carnivorous mammals.

BIBLIOGRAPHY

Clutton-Brock, J. *Domesticated Animals from Early Times.* Austin: University of Texas Press, 1981.

Crisler, Lois. *Arctic Wild.* Boston: Little, Brown, 1968.

———. *Captive Wild.* Boston: Little, Brown, 1969.

Dobie, L. Frank. *The Voice of the Coyote.* Lincoln: University of Nebraska Press, 1961.

Fiennes, R. *The Order of Wolves.* Indianapolis: Bobbs-Merrill, 1976.

Fiennes, R., and A. Fiennes. *The Natural History of the Dog.* New York: Doubleday, 1969.

Fuller, J. L., and J. P. Scott. *Genetics and the Social Behavior of the Dog.* Chicago: University of Chicago Press, 1965.

Leydet, F. *The Coyote: Defiant Songdog of the West.* Norman: University of Oklahoma Press, 1977.

Lorenz, K. *Man Meets Dog.* Baltimore: Penguin, 1973.

———. *On Aggression.* New York: Harcourt, Brace & World, 1963.

Mech, L. David. *The Wolf: Ecology and Behavior of an Endangered Species.* New York: Natural History Press, 1970.

Mowat, F. *Never Cry Wolf.* New York: Dell, 1977.

Romer, A. S. *Vertebrate Paleontology.* Chicago: University of Chicago Press, 1966.

Ryden, Hope. *God's Dog: A Celebration of the North American Coyote.* New York: Viking, 1979.

Smythe, R. H. *The Dog: Structure and Movement.* New York: Arco, 1970.

Vaughan, T. A. *Mammalogy.* Philadelphia: Saunders, 1972.

Ucko, Peter J., and G. W. Dimbleby, eds. *The Domestication and Exploitation of Plants and Animals.* New York: Aldine-Atherton, 1969.

Young, J. Z. *The Life of Mammals.* New York: Oxford University Press, 1975.

Each of these works lists its own detailed bibliography, from which more technical information may be gleaned.

INDEX

achondroplasia, 124–25, 127, 129
acromegaly, 108–11, 112, 113, 114, 116
Aeluroides, 25–26
  body markings of, 26
  exclusive carnivory of, 27, 42
  social hunting among, 60–61
  stalking by, 26, 41, 49, 58
  three families of, 26
Aesop, 45
Afghan hound, x, 100, 102, 103, 104
Africa, 19, 30, 37, 50, 51, 52, 54, 60, 61, 63, 64, 65, 73–74, 91, 94, 97, 99, 121, 131
agriculture
  canoid adaptability to, 27, 32, 46–47, 121
  and functions of domestic canid, 105, 108, 119, 120–21
Airedale, 46, 119, 120, 121
akita, 94
Alaska, 81
Alaskan malamute, 96. *See also* malamute
Alopex, 143
Alopex lagopus, 53
alpha male, 55
Amazon foxes, 55, 57
American Kennel Club, 136
Amphicyon, 42
anal gland, canid, 37, 40
Andean wild dog, 55
animal-baiting, 119, 122–23
Antarctica, ix, 44, 69
antelope, 36, 65, 66, 74, 98, 100, 102, 137, 138
Anubis, 74
Arab wolf, 91, 97
Arctic Circle, 53, 90, 96
Arctic fox, 53–54, 142
Arctocyonidae, 21, 22
Argentina, 55
arousal ceremony, 65
arthropods, 56
Asia, 30, 45, 50, 54, 66, 67, 71, 74, 75, 79, 81, 88, 89, 90, 91, 96, 97, 98, 99, 114
Asian wolf, 88, 91, 97
Assyria, 108
Atelocynus, 143
Atelocynus microtus, 57
auditory bullae, 30
aurochs, 90
Australia, ix, 19–21, 44, 50, 87, 88, 94, 97, 123
Australopithecus africanus, 65–66
Aztecs, 117, 119

baboon, 66
badger, 30, 32, 137, 138
badger-hound, 112–13
baleen whale, 61
bark, canid, 42, 71, 85, 98
basenji, 98, 99, 119
Basques, 110, 114
Bassariscus astutus, 32
basset hound, 113, 128, 129
bat, 3, 4, 6, 21
bat-eared fox, 51–52, 54, 144
beagle, 113
bear, 30, 32, 35, 36, 41, 42, 59, 120
bear-dog, 42

Bengali fox, 50, 142
Beowulf, 80
bipeds, 6, 66
birds, 3, 6, 8, 16, 47, 52, 53, 54, 114, 134
  in Paleocene, 11
bison, 70, 75, 76
black-and-tan coonhound, 113
black-and-white sheepdog, 93
black-backed jackal, 73–74, 144
Blanford's fox, 51, 142
bloodhound, 93, 111–14, 131
blue whale, 4
bobcat, 27
body-cooling system, in canids, 37, 100
body markings
  canid, 42, 64–65, 67, 93
  of killer whale, 60
borhyaenid "dog," 20
Borhyaenidae, 20
borzoi, 102
Boston bullterrier, 128
boxer, 123, 124
brain. *See also* intelligence
  canid, xii, 9, 17, 37, 93, 117, 136
  of condylarth, 21
  contrasted in wolf and domestic dog, 93
  of creodont, 23
  human, 17
  of miacids, 23
  of primitive mammals, 8–9
  and socialization of herbivores, 59
breeds, domestic. *See also Canis familiaris*; domestication; selective breeding; and under individual breeds
  dwarf, 96, 106, 113, 114, 124–29
  early phylogeny of, 94–104
  fighting, 119, 122–24
  of gazehound descent, 98–104, 105, 110
  genetic classification of, xii, 136
  genetic patterns in, x, 92–93, 96, 97, 102, 106, 109, 113, 114, 119, 127, 139
  giant, 106–11, 131
  midget, 116–24
  mutational influence on, 105–11, 112, 113, 114, 116–17, 121, 124–25, 127, 129
  number of, 136
  oldest purebred, 99
  pariah-dingo stock of, 97–98, 106, 109, 119, 133
  "primitive" polar, 94–97, 105, 109, 115, 117, 119
  purebred vs. mongrel, 139–41
  scent-tracking group of, 111–14
  sporting, 114–15
British Isles, 81, 109, 119, 129, 140
brown bear, 35
bullbaiting, 123
bulldog, 85, 119, 123, 124, 129
bullterrier, 122, 123, 124, 128
bush dog, 55–56, 144
"butterfly-lion," 125

cacomistle, 32
camel, 91
Canada, 50, 70, 81, 110, 111
Canidae. *See also* genera and species
  adaptability of, ix, 46–47, 50, 52–53, 55, 69, 73, 76, 83, 92, 99, 102, 115, 136, 139–40, 141
  compared to Ursidae, 35
  cursorial life-style of, xii, 35–37, 38, 41, 42, 44, 55, 62, 78, 80, 98, 100–104, 111, 112, 113–14, 137–38
  descent from *Tomarctus*, 42
  ears of, *see* ears, canid
  evolutionary endpoint of, 69, 73
  extinct forms of, ix, 40–44, 55
  feet and legs of, 35, 37, 55, 63, 100, 102, 108, 125, 129
  genera and species of, ix, 44, 142–44
  geographical range of, ix, 44, 69, 70
  as homogeneous family, ix, 17, 46, 72, 105–106
  intelligence of, *see* intelligence
  jaws of, *see* jaws
  largest species of, 75
  miacid ancestry of, 25, 59
  natural selection of, xii, 38, 48, 87, 89–90, 91, 105–106, 110, 134, 136, 141
  nose of, 10, 37, 40, 100. *See also* smell, sense of
  place in superfamily, 30
  as predators, vii, xi, xii, 17, 27, 35–36, 41, 53, 58, 62, 63, 65–67, 75–79, 85–86, 92, 98, 104, 119, 121–22, 134–35
  skeleton of, 38–39, 88, 93, 100, 106, 108, 116–17, 124–25, 129
  skin glands of, 37, 40
  skull of, 63, 85, 86, 89, 96, 108
  social hunting by, 17, 41, 48, 55, 62, 64, 65, 67, 73–74, 76, 86, 92, 98, 134–35
  socialization and loyalty among, viii–ix, 17, 41–42, 52, 53, 62–63, 64, 67, 73, 82, 98, 110, 112, 120, 130, 140–41
  South American, 54–57, 142–44
  species of largest range and numbers, 83
  symbiosis with man, vii–viii, ix–xii, 10, 17, 18, 27, 44, 47–48, 52–53, 56, 69, 73, 77–78, 82, 83–92, 94, 96–97, 98, 100, 102–104, 105–106, 108, 110–12,

Canidae (*continued*)
114, 122–27, 130–41
teeth of, *see* molar teeth, teeth
vegetarian capability of, 23, 27, 30, 47, 98
vision of, *see* vision
"viverrid kill" of, 25
voice of, 42, 71, 78–79, 85, 91, 98, 112, 132
wild, viii–ix, 27, 40, 45–57, 58–68, 69–82, 83, 84, 85–87, 88, 89, 91, 92, 98, 105–106, 130, 134, 139, 141
Canis, 46, 69–82, 143. *See also* species
central type of, 75
considered as species rather than genus, 73
feral forms of, 88, 97–98, 105, 134
nine species of, 69, 144
social structure of, 73, 82
taxonomic problems of, 69–73, 75, 83–84, 88, 90, 91
Canis adustus, 73, 144
Canis aureus, 74, 144
Canis dingo, 88, 144. *See also* dingo
Canis familiaris, vii–xiii, 3, 17, 18, 25, 44, 55, 58, 62, 67, 69, 83–93, 94–104, 105–15, 116–29, 130–41, 144. *See also* breeds, domestic; domestication; selective breeding; and under individual breeds
breeding cycle of, 98, 134
coloring genes of, 92–93, 97
companionship of, viii, x–xii, 17, 53, 96, 122, 126, 130, 131, 138–41
considered as "race" rather than species, 73, 88
contrasted with tame wolf, 87
diversity of, xii, 71–72, 84, 90, 91, 92–93, 99–100, 105–106, 112, 130–31, 136
early forms of, 88–92, 94, 96–104, 105–106, 108, 110–12, 117, 119, 125
first departure from wolf ancestry of, 98–100, 102
as food, 98, 117, 119, 130, 132–34, 136
illustrative of taxonomic anomalies, 71–72
as infant surrogate, 127, 138
interbreeding with wild canid, x, 71, 88, 106
jaw changes of, 85–86, 89–90, 108, 110, 123, 124, 129
as laboratory animal, 132, 134
physical contrast with wild canids, 84–86, 88–89, 97–98, 100, 125
range and numbers of, 83, 133, 136
split personality of, 130–35
Canis familiaris inostranzewi, 90
Canis familiaris intermedius, 90
Canis familiaris matris-optimae, 90
Canis familiaris palustris, 90
Canis latrans, 69, 73, 144. *See also* coyote
Canis lupus, 73, 75, 79, 82, 144. *See also* wolf
Canis lupus arabs, 91, 97
Canis lupus laniger, 106
Canis lupus lupus, 91
Canis lupus pallipes, 88, 91, 97
Canis mesomelas, 73, 144
Canis niger, 70, 144
Canis simensis, 75, 144
Canoidea, 25–26
four families of, 30–35
omnivory of, 27, 30, 32, 35
Cape hunting dog, 37, 63–66, 67, 73, 144
Cape silver fox, 51, 142
carnassial teeth, 14, 21, 22, 23–24, 25, 35, 63, 85, 86
Carnivora, 15, 19, 21, 32, 72, 91. *See also* carnivores
taxonomy of, 19, 21, 25–26, 30, 32
carnivores, mammalian, xii, 3, 12–18, 19–26. *See also* Aeluroides; Canidae; Canoidea; Fissipeda; predators
claws of, 14–15
contrast of dog and cat as, 27, 30
education and bonding among, 16–17, 49
extinct orders, suborders, and families of, 21–25
family tree of, 28–29, 30
feral, 88, 97–98, 134
intelligence of, 15–16
marsupial, 19–21, 54–55
modern suborders and superfamilies of, 19, 21, 25–26, 27, 30
most successful family among, 44
number of genera of, 19
prehuman remnants among, 67
social hunting by, 16, 17
teeth of, 12–14
territorialism of, 17–18
toes of, 14, 19, 35, 42, 63
cat, domestic, ix, xii, 18, 25–26, 46, 119, 139
compared to terrier as mouser, 121
feral, 134
red fox compared to, 48–49
cats, wild, 23, 25–26, 27, 54, 61, 66, 73, 77, 78. *See also* Aeluroides
contrasted with canoids in agricultural ecosystems, 30, 47
most specialized carnivores, 26
solitary hunters, 41

cattle, 36, 86, 90, 123, 131
Celts, 80, 100, 109
Cenozoic era, 6, 11, 15, 19–20, 21
Cerdocyon, 143
Cerdocyon thous, 56, 142, 144
cerebrum, of primitive mammals, 8–9
Cernunnos, 80
"chasing" response, 100, 103
cheekbone
  in acromegalic breeds, 108
  canid, 89–90
  mammalian, 7
cheetah, 114
Chihuahua, 84, 117, 118, 119
Chile, 55
China, 32, 54, 81, 97, 125, 127, 133, 134, 136
Chinese "crested" dog, 119
chow, 94–95, 97, 109, 125, 132–33
chromosomes, 46, 91
Chrysocyon, 143
Chrysocyon brachyurus, 55, 144
clan. *See also* socialization
  of carnivores, 17
  wolf, 79
coach dog, 93, 114, 115
coati, 32, 35
cock-a-poo, 129
cocker spaniel, 114, 129
collarbone, of *Lycaon*, 63
collie, 102–103, 117
colonialism
  of Arctic fox, 53
  of fennec fox, 52
color phases
  of Arctic fox, 53
  of red fox, 49
  of wolf, 79
coloring genes, in domestic dog, 92–93
Columbus, Christopher, 90
communication, canid. *See also* socialization
  in body markings, 42, 64
  with man, ix, xii, 42, 79, 112, 131, 140
  through pinnae, 10
  "semaphore" system of, 10, 42, 84
  through skin glands, 37, 40
  in social hunting, 16, 41–42, 60–61
  vocal, 42, 71, 78–79, 91, 112, 132
Condylarthra, 21, 22, 24
coonhound, 113
corgi, 128, 129
corsac fox, 50, 142
coursing, 99, 104
coyote, x, 27, 40, 45, 69–71, 72, 74, 87, 90, 134, 144
  contrasted with true wolf, 70
  interbreeding with wolf, 70–71
  regarded as "race" rather than species, 73
crab-eating fox, 56, 142
crab-eating raccoon, 32
crayfish, 54
Creodonta, 21, 23, 24, 28
Cretaceous period, 19
Crocuta crocuta, 60
cross fox, 49
culpeo fox, 55, 142
Cuon, 143
Cuon alpinus, 66, 144

dachshund, x, 71–72, 93, 112–13, 129, 137–38
Dalmatian, 93, 114, 115
deer, vii, 23, 36, 67, 75, 78, 102, 135, 140
deerhound, 100, 102, 110
Denmark, 90
dhole, 66–68, 144
Diatryma, 11
Didelphis virginiana, 20
dingo, 20, 72, 87, 88, 90, 91, 97, 98, 105, 106, 119, 131, 133, 144
dinosaurs
  and mammals, 7–9, 10, 11, 15, 59
  social hunting by, 60
  and synapsids, 6–7
disease, canid, 74, 110
Doberman pinscher, 93, 117, 132, 140
Dobermann, Ludwig, 132
dogfighting, 119, 122–24
dolichocephaly, 99–100
domestic dog: *see* breeds, domestic; *Canis familiaris*; domestication
domestication, 83–93
  influence on canid intelligence, 110, 112, 134
  origins of, vii–viii, xii, 73, 83, 86–92, 94, 96–99, 105
  physical characteristics of, 84–85, 89–90, 92–93, 98, 99–100, 102, 105–12, 114, 116–19, 123–27, 129, 137–39
  purposes and functions of, viii, ix–x, xii, 87, 91, 93, 96, 98, 100, 102, 104, 105–106, 111–12, 114–15, 117, 119–124, 130–33, 137–41
Doyle, A. Conan, 130
dromaeosaur, 60
Dusicyon, 55, 142, 143
Dusicyon australis, 55
Dusicyon culpaeus, 55, 142
Dusicyon griseus, 55, 142
Dusicyon inca, 55, 142
dwarfing, 96, 106, 113, 114, 124–27, 129

eagle, 53
ears, canid, x, 9–10, 30, 88
in acromegalic dogs, 108, 111, 112, 114
contrast in wild and domestic canids, 84, 93, 96
cropping of, 132
heat radiation by, 50, 51
as organs of expression, 10
in polar breeds, 84, 90
Egypt, 74, 98, 99, 100, 114, 119, 125, 136
elephant, 59, 64, 77, 91, 110
elk, 75
elkhound, 93, 96
endothermy, 3, 7
energy efficiency
canid, 35
of dinosaurs, 6, 7
mammalian, 4, 6, 7, 17
England, 81, 119, 126, 140
English bulldog, 123, 129
English mastiff, 109, 110
English toy spaniel, 127
Eocene epoch, 12, 21, 23, 26
Eskimos, 79, 130
ethology, 82, 91
Eurasia, 19, 30, 32, 45, 50, 54, 75, 77, 78, 88, 89, 90, 94, 100
Europe, 47, 54, 64, 75, 80, 81, 89, 90, 96, 102, 108, 110, 115, 119, 127, 130
evolution
of Canidae, 27, 30, 40–44, 51, 55, 65, 69, 75, 94, 105–106
and classification of breeds, xii, 94, 136
convergent, 21, 58, 74, 137–38
diversity in canid, 49, 55, 94, 105–106, 136, 139
of domestic dog, 83–93, 94–104, 105–115, 116–29, 130–31, 136–39
human, 65–66, 75, 77, 105
of insectivorous mammals, 7–11, 12
interaction of herbivores and predators in, 58–59
of mammalian (placental) carnivores, 12–18, 21–26, 59
of marsupial carnivores, 19–21
mutants and, 105–106, 108, 109, 110, 112, 113, 114, 116–17, 124–27, 129
and process of domestication, vii–viii, 17, 58, 94, 130–31
of synapsids, 5–6
of wolf, 75–77

Falkland Islands dog, 55
Felidae, 26, 29
three genera of, 44
Felis, 44
Felis concolor, 27
fennec fox, 10, 52, 144
Fennecus, 143
Fennecus zerda, 52, 144
ferret, 32, 121, 122
fisher, 32
Fissipeda, 19, 21, 25
Flehmen, 40
fox, 10, 27, 37, 42, 45–57, 67, 119, 121, 141. *See also* red fox
contrasted with true dog, 73
contrasted with wild dog, 58, 62
domestication of, 52–53, 56
human exploitation of, 47, 48, 50, 53, 57
stealth-hunting by, 48, 49, 58
taxonomy of, 46, 50, 51, 142
fox hunt, 48, 50, 119
fox terrier, 48, 121, 139
foxhound, 48, 113
Fuegians, 133, 136
fur, 3, 7, 8, 30
of chow, 97
fox, 47, 48, 50, 53
of raccoon dog, 54
"furbearers," 3

game animals, 47, 78, 79, 81, 83, 98, 104, 114, 134, 140
gazehound, 92, 98–104, 105, 106, 111, 114
genet, 25
genetics, human manipulation of, 136–137. *See also* breeds, domestic; selective breeding
German shepherd, x, 84, 93, 96, 140
Germany, 132
giant panda, 32
giant sloth, 91
gigantism
canid, 106–11, 131
canoid, 30, 35
among herbivores, 58–59, 62, 77, 78
glaciation, 64, 75, 80, 88, 96
glutton, 30
goat, 36, 131
golden jackal, 74–75, 144
and ancestry of domestic dog, 91, 99
gray fox, 50, 51, 142
Great Dane, 71–72, 110
Great Pyrenees, 109, 110
Greece, 81, 102, 108
greyhound, 93, 99, 100, 102, 103, 117, 137–38
grouse, 47
guard dogs, viii, 97, 103, 106, 108, 110, 119, 131, 132, 133
Gulo luscus, 30

harefoot fox, 53
hares, 55, 139
harrier, 113
hawk, 114
hearing, sense of
  of canids, 10
  of dinosaurs, 8
  of first mammals, 8, 9, 16
  of primates, 9
heart patients, dogs and, ix–x
herbivores, 15, 16, 21, 23, 27, 35, 55, 67, 74, 85, 86, 98
  domestication of, 79, 96, 106, 131
  interaction with canids, 15, 36, 58–59, 70, 75–76
  marsupial, 20
  size increase of, 58–59, 62, 77, 78
herders, viii, 87, 88, 90, 91, 93, 96, 98, 102–103, 106, 134. *See also* sheep-dogs
herds, predators and, 15, 16, 59, 62, 65, 78, 85, 86–87, 106, 134
Hesperocyon, 42, 43
hippopotamus, 64
Holarctic brown bear, 30
Homo sapiens
  blood sports of, 119, 122–24
  body cooling of, 37
  and competing intelligences, ix, 45, 47–48, 50, 57, 62, 70, 75, 78, 81–82, 130, 133
  consumption of canine flesh, 98, 117, 119, 130, 132–34, 136
  dogs directed against, 111–12, 130, 131–32, 135
  first city-states of, 105
  folklore of wolves, 78–81
  as hunter, xii, 48, 50, 58, 61–62, 74, 76, 77–80, 81–82, 83, 85–87, 88, 90–91, 98, 102, 104, 114, 135, 140
  influence on canoid ecosystems, xii, 27, 32, 46–47, 49–50, 67, 69–70, 74, 78, 79
  nomadic, 94, 96
  omnivory of, 14, 30
  and Reynard, 45, 47–49, 57
  running speed compared to canid, 62, 112
  symbiosis with canids, vii–viii, ix–xii, 10, 17, 18, 27, 52–53, 58, 65, 69, 73, 77–80, 82, 83–92, 94, 96–97, 98, 100, 102–104, 105–106, 108, 110–12, 114, 119–21, 122–27, 130–41
  teeth of, 14, 15
  use of bloodhound by, 111–12, 131
hoofed mammals, 21, 23
horse, 23, 36, 48, 91
hound, xii, 100, 112–14
Hound of the Baskervilles, The (Doyle), 130, 135
Humane Society of the United States, 133
Hungary, 81
hunting
  and convergent evolution, 137–38
  cursorial, xii, 35, 36–37, 38, 41, 55, 62, 78, 99–100, 102, 111–12, 113–14, 137–38
  interaction of wolf and human, 75–80, 83, 85–86, 88, 90, 130
  origin of human-canid symbiosis, viii, xii, 58, 86–87, 90–91, 96, 98–100, 137
  sight-hunting, by canids, 65, 92, 98, 100
  social, by Aeluroides, 60–61
  social, by canids, 17, 41, 48, 55, 62, 64, 65, 67, 73–74, 76, 86, 88, 92, 98, 134–135
  social, by carnivores, 16, 59–61
  social, by dinosaurs, 60
  "sport," by humans, 81–82
  stealth-hunting, by cats, 16, 26, 41, 58
  stealth-hunting, by foxes, 48, 49, 58
hunting dogs, domestic, viii, xii, 48, 96, 133. *See also* wild hunting dogs
  converge with prey, 137–38
  gazehound group of, 98–104
  lurcher as, 140
  mastiff as, 110
  terrier as, 48, 119–21
husky, 72, 83, 84, 87, 90, 93, 96
Hyaenidae, 26, 29
Hyaenodontidae, 23, 24, 28
hyena, 61, 66, 73
hyena dog, 64

Idaho, 90
Inca fox, 55, 142
India, 45, 66, 67, 97, 98, 106, 108
Indian desert fox, 50, 142
Indians, American, 79, 91
"inner space," 9
insectivores, 6, 7, 8–9, 10, 12, 52, 91
insects, 58, 136
intelligence
  canid, ix, x, xii, 5, 15, 18, 44, 45, 47, 57, 82, 88, 92, 98, 110, 115, 140, 141
  of carnivores, 15–18
  domestication and, 110, 112, 134
  mammalian, 5, 8
interbreeding. *See also* selective breeding
  of domestic races, 92, 94, 109, 110, 114, 127, 129, 131, 132, 139, 140
  of species, x, 69, 70–71, 83–84, 91, 96, 106

interdigital glands, canid, 37
Ireland, 81, 119
Irish setter, 92, 115
Irish wolfhound, 103, 110
Israel, 90
Italian greyhound, 117
Italy, 81, 102, 108

jackal, 56, 71, 72, 73–74, 91, 99, 141, 144
jackrabbit, 104, 139
Jacobson's organs, 40
Japan, 54
Japanese spaniel, 114
jaw joint, mammalian, 4, 7
jaws
  in acromegalic dog, 108, 110
  canid, 36, 42, 139
  changes in domestic dog, 89–90, 129
  contrast in wolf and domestic dog, 85, 86
  in fighting dog, 123, 124, 129
  of insectivores, 12
  of synapsids, 6
  of wild dog, 62, 63
Jericho, 47

kangaroo, 88
keeshond, 96
kennel clubs, 123, 136
killer whales, 60, 61
killing technique
  canid, 25, 62, 65, 85, 119, 122
  of miacids, 24–25
  with small prey, 58
  viverrid, 25
  of weasels, 32
kinkajou, 35
kit fox, 50, 51, 142
"knife" teeth: *see* carnassial teeth
komondor, 110
Kuvasczok, 110

Labrador retriever, 92, 115
lagamorphs, 23
linsang, 25
lion, 61, 62, 110, 120
"lion-dog," 97, 125
live birth, 19
lizards, 7
lop-ear, 84, 93, 132
Lord of the Rings (Tolkien), 136
Lorenz, Konrad, vii, 91
lurcher, 140–41
lycanthropy, 80
Lycaon, 63–64, 143
Lycaon anglicus, 64
Lycaon pictus, 64, 66, 144
Lynx, 44
Lynx rufus, 27

Madagascar, 30
malamute, 83, 84, 94, 96
Malay sun bear, 35
Maltese dogs, 96, 117, 119
Maltese dwarf, 94
mammals, 3–11. *See also* carnivores, mammalian
  education among, 16
  evolution in size, 58–59
  extinction of northern giants among, 77–78
  first, 6, 7–11, 58–59
  jaw-joint position in, 4–5, 7
  marsupial, 19–21, 54–55, 88
  placental, 19, 20, 21, 51, 55, 88
  primate divergence among, 9–10
mammoth, imperial, 76
Man Meets Dog (Lorenz), vii
Manchester terrier, 117, 132
maned wolf, 55, 56, 144
Maori, 133
marsupial wolf, 20, 21, 88
marsupials, 19–21, 54–55, 88
marten, 30, 32
mastiff, 84, 108–12, 114, 115, 116, 127, 129
Mech, L. David, 75
megalosaur, 60
Mesocyon, 40–42
Mesolithic age, 87
Mesonychidae, 21, 22
Mesozoic era, 7, 9, 10–11, 12, 16, 21
Mexican hairless dog, 117, 118
Mexico, 32, 50, 75, 81, 117
Miacidae, 23–25, 26, 28, 30, 59
Miacis, 25
midget races, of domestic dog, 98, 102–103, 115, 116–19, 121, 124
Miocene epoch, 29
molar teeth
  canid, 42
  in carnivores, 13, 14
  of dhole, 67
  in early insectivores, 12, 13
  in *Homo sapiens*, 13, 14
  of procyonids, 32
  in red fox, 49
  reduced in bush dog, 55–56
  shearing function of, in creodonts, 23, 24
  ursid, 35
  of wild dog, 62
Molossian, 108
mongoose, 25, 61

mongrel, x, 139–41
monkey, 32, 45, 64
mottling, 64
mousers, 121
musk-oxen, 76
Mustela rixosa, 30
Mustelidae, 29, 30–32
mutants, canid, 105–11, 112, 113, 114, 116–17, 121, 124–27, 129
muzzle-bite, ritual, 42, 87, 139

Nasua, 35
Neolithic age, 47, 89, 96, 98
neopallium, 9, 10, 17
neoteny, 84–85
Netherlands, 96
New Mexico, x, 104
New Zealand, 50
Newfoundland dog, 110, 111, 115
nocturnalism
  of bush dog, 55, 56
  of dingo, 88
  of early mammals, 6, 7–9
  of fox, 48
  of hyena, 61, 66
  of weasel, 30
Norsemen, 80
North America, 19, 21, 27, 30, 32, 42, 44, 45, 47, 50, 54, 55, 69–70, 73, 75, 78, 81, 90, 113, 123, 130
northern wolf, 91
Norwegian elkhound, 93
Norwegian husky, 96
Nyctereutes, 143
Nyctereutes procyonoides, 54, 144

omnivory
  canoid capability of, 23, 27, 30, 32, 35, 42, 44, 49, 50
  tool-using, 14
opossum, American, 20, 54
Oppian, 119
orbital angle, 89
Orcinus, 60
Osteoborus, 42, 43
Otocyon, 143
Otocyon megalotis, 51
Oxyaenidae, 21, 23, 28

packs, 17, 41–42, 48, 55, 62–63, 64, 65, 66, 73, 79, 87, 98, 131, 134–35. *See also* hunting; socialization
Paleocene epoch, 11, 12, 16, 19, 21, 23, 59
pampas fox, 55, 142
Panama, Isthmus of, 54
Pangaea, 20
Panthera, 44
panting, 37
papillon, 114, 117
pariah dogs, 90, 91, 97–98, 99, 105, 106, 108, 119, 131, 133
Peke-a-poo, 127
Pekingese, x, 116, 125–27, 138, 140
Persia, 90
pharaoh hound, 119, 120
pheromones, 37
Phoenicians, 109
pinnae, 9–10
Pinnipedia, 19, 21, 32
pit bullterrier, 123–24
pituitary gland, 106, 108, 117
Pleistocene epoch, 29, 64, 75–76, 77
Pliocene epoch, 23, 29
poaching, 140
pointer, 83, 93, 114, 115
polar bear, 35, 53
polar dogs, 83, 84, 90, 94–96, 98, 102, 103, 105, 106, 108, 115, 117, 119, 129
polecat, 32, 121
Polynesians, 133
Pomeranian, 96, 117
Pompeii, 135, 136
poodle, 115, 117, 127, 129
pouched dog, 20
"prairie wolf," 69
predators
  birds as, 11, 16, 53
  canids as, vii, xii, 17, 27, 35–36, 53, 58, 62, 63, 65–67, 75–76, 92, 98, 134–35
  carnivorous, 12, 14–18, 19–26, 27, 30, 32, 53, 59–60
  contrast of cat and dog as, 16, 26, 27, 36, 41, 58
  contrast of fox and wild dog as, 58, 62
  dinosaurs as, 7–8, 15, 60
  extinct orders of mammalian, 21, 23–26
  and herbivores, 15, 16, 20, 21, 23, 27, 36, 55, 58–60, 65, 67, 70, 75–76, 77, 85–86, 91, 98
  intelligent, ix, 15–18, 45, 47, 57, 88
  marsupial, 18–21, 54–55, 88
  most efficient canid, 75–79
  and shepherd dog, 106, 120
  social groups of, 17, 41–42, 55, 59–62, 73–74, 76, 86, 88, 98, 134–35
  synapsids as, 15
premammals, 4
primates, ix, 9, 10, 37, 61
Procyon cancrivorous, 32
Procyon lotor, 32
Procyonidae, 29, 30, 32, 35, 36, 40
pug, 85, 127
puma, 27

pups
  and artificial selection, 116, 124
  births of, in U.S., 133
  Doberman, 132
  ears of, 84
  trained for blood sports, 123–24
  of wild dogs and wolves, 62–63, 64, 65, 84, 85, 87
pygmies: *see* midget races, of domestic dog

rabbit, 23, 47, 49, 100, 102, 104, 113, 139
raccoon, 27, 32, 35, 54
raccoon dog, 54, 144
racing, dog, 102
rats, ix, 24, 119, 121, 134, 136
ratting, 122
red dog, 66
red fox, 45–50, 56, 57, 116, 142
  and agricultural ecosystems, 47–48
  color phases of, 49
  mating and family of, 49
  mythology of, 45
  range of, 48, 49–50
red wolf, 70, 144
reindeer, 75, 86
reptiles, 4, 11, 52
rescue dogs, 110, 111
rete mirabile, 37
retriever, 114–15
  Airedale functioning as, 120
rhinoceros, 77
Rhodesian Ridgeback, 131
Rin Tin Tin, 130
ring-tailed cat, 32
ritual grooming, 42, 52, 54
rodents, 58
Romulus and Remus, 80
ruff, 42, 96, 97
Rufus (author's dog), x–xii, 87, 139
running
  canid, xii, 14, 35–37, 38, 41, 42, 44, 55, 62, 80, 111, 112, 113–14, 121–22
  of gazehound, 98–104
  of *Mesocyon*, 4
  of thylacine, 88
  of *Tomarctus*, 42
Russia, 102
Russian wolfhound, 102

saber-toothed cats, 23
Sahara, 51, 52
Saint Bernard, 109
saluki, 99, 100, 102, 104
Samoyed, 92, 94, 96, 97
"sand shoes," 52
sauropods, 60
Scandinavia, 81, 90, 96
scavenging, 42, 49, 53, 56, 61, 73, 74, 76
  and origins of domestication, 86, 97
scent: *see* smell, sense of
scent-hound, 111–12
schipperke, 94
Scotland, 81, 119
Scottish terrier, 128, 129
sea lion, 19, 32
sea otter, 30, 32
seal, 19, 32
Seckenberg dog, 90
Seeing Eye dog, 114
selective breeding, x, 92–93, 94, 96–100, 102, 104, 106, 109, 110, 111–14, 116–17, 119, 121–24, 125–27, 129, 131, 132, 136–38
  vs. mutts, 139–41
setter, 92, 93, 114, 140
shark, 65
shearing teeth: *see* carnassial teeth
sheep, xi, 86, 88, 93, 103, 131, 134
sheepdogs, 88, 90, 93, 96, 102, 106, 117, 131, 134, 140. *See also* herders
shepherd dog, 72, 84, 91, 92, 110, 120, 129, 130, 131
  distinguished from sheepdog, 106
Shetland sheepdog, 102, 117
Shih Tzu, 127
showdogs, 123, 139
shrew, 16, 91
Siberian husky, 96. *See also* husky
sickle tail, 84
side-striped jackal, 73–74, 144
Simocyon, 42
Simpson, George Gaylord, 21
skunk, 32
small-eared fox, 56–57
smell, sense of
  of canids, 10, 37, 40, 111
  of first mammals, 8–9, 16
social hunting: *see* hunting; socialization
socialization
  among Canidae, viii–ix, 17, 37, 41–42, 52, 53, 55, 62–63, 64, 65, 67, 69, 70, 73, 88, 130
  of carnivores, 17
  of coatis, 32
  of herbivores, 16, 59
  key factor in domestication, 17, 73, 87, 110
  of *Mesocyon*, 41–42
  in organized hunting, 16, 17, 41, 55, 59–61, 62, 65, 73, 76, 86, 88, 92, 98, 134–35
  skin glands and, 37

within genus *Canis*, 69, 73, 76, 80, 82, 83, 84, 86, 87
South America, 19–20, 32, 35, 50, 54–56, 133
southern Asian wolf, 88, 91, 97
Soviet Union, 81
spaniel, 92, 114, 115, 127, 129
specialization
arboreal, 9, 10, 32, 35
of carnivores, 12–18, 26, 30, 67
in cats, 26, 49
deficits of, 110, 112, 127, 138
of domestic canids, viii, xii, 73, 90, 92, 93, 96, 97, 98–104, 105–106, 108, 112, 113, 114–15, 116–17, 119–29, 136–38
early mammalian, 7–11
of ears for heat radiation, 50, 51
human, 91, 105
of nocturnal mammals, 7, 8
of poodle, 115
for running speed and endurance, 35–37, 38, 41, 42, 44, 55, 62, 80, 98–104, 111, 112, 113, 120, 121
of size, 7, 30, 35, 50, 58–59, 70, 77–78, 96, 98, 102, 106, 108, 113, 116–17, 121–22, 124–27, 129
of small foxes, 51–53
vegetarian, among carnivores, 27, 32, 35, 42
in wild dogs, 62, 73
within genus *Canis*, 69–70, 73, 90, 91
Speothos, 143
Speothos venaticus, 55, 144
spider, 116
spitz, 96
sporting breeds, xii, 114
spotted hyena, 60–61
spotting, 64–65, 93
spotting-dogs, 114
springer spaniel, 114
stalking
by cats, 16, 26, 48, 49
contrasted with canid running, 36, 41
by foxes, 48–49, 58
stilt fox, 55
supracaudal gland: *see* tail
swift fox, 50
Switzerland, 90
synapsids, 5–7, 15, 19

tail, canid
contrast in wild and domestic dogs, 84, 97
helical, 85
as "semaphore," 42, 84
supracaudal gland of, 37
Tasmania, 20, 88
Tasmanian devil, 21
taxonomy
of Canidae, 142, 144
of Canoidea, 30
of Carnivora, 19, 21, 25–26, 30
and genus *Canis*, 69–73, 75, 83–84, 88, 90, 91, 144
teeth
of bat-eared fox, 51–52
of bush dog, 55–56
canid, vii, 12–14, 15, 23, 42, 62, 63, 67, 85, 89
"canine," 12–14, 21, 23, 85
carnassial, *see* carnassial teeth
of condylarths, 21
of creodonts, 23
human, 12–14
of insectivores, 12–14
of miacids, 23–24, 25
molar, *see* molar teeth
of Pekingese, 127
procyonid, 32
ursid, 35
terrier, 24, 90, 93, 119–23, 128, 129, 132, 139, 140
territorialism, 17–18, 49–50
therapsids, 6
thylacine, 20, 21, 88
Tibet, 106
Tibetan fox, 50, 142
Tibetan mastiff, 106
Tibetan spaniel, 114
Tierra del Fuego, 90
tiger, 67
"tiger" borhyaenids, 20
timber wolf, 70
Tolkien, J.R.R., 136–37
Tomarctus, 42, 43, 143
totems, 80
toy breeds, xii, 84, 103, 119, 127, 129. *See also* dwarfing; midget races, of domestic dog
convergent evolution and, 138
toy poodle, 117, 127, 129
toy spaniel, 114, 127
tracking, 8–10, 16. *See also* hunting; stalking
by bloodhound, 111–12, 131
trapping, 47, 48, 53
Triassic period, 7
tribes: *see* packs; socialization
trot, canid, 62, 96
tympanic bone, 30

United States, disposal of dogs in, 133–34, 136
urine, 40

Urocyon, 50
Ursidae, 29, 30, 35
Ursus arctos, 30
uselessness-related disease, dogs and, ix–x

vertebrates, 5, 7, 8, 15, 60, 106
"violet" gland, 37
vision
  canid, 10
  color, 9
  in first mammals, 8, 9, 16
  in foxes, 48–49
  and hunting, 65, 92, 98, 100
  in primates, 9
"viverrid kill," 25
Viverridae, 25, 26, 29, 30
Vulpes, 45–51, 142, 143
Vulpes bengalensis, 50, 142
Vulpes canus, 51, 142
Vulpes cinereoargentatus, 50, 142
Vulpes corsac, 50, 142
Vulpes ferrilatus, 50, 142
Vulpes leucopus, 50, 142
Vulpes velox, 50, 142
Vulpes vulpes, 45, 46, 142. *See also* red fox

Wales, 64, 119, 129
walking
  digitigrade, 35, 36
  plantigrade, 32, 35, 36
wallaby, 4
walrus, 19, 32
war dogs, viii, 106, 108, 110, 114, 131
water spaniel, 114
weasel, 30–32, 35, 121
weimaraner, 93
Welsh sheepdog, 103
werewolves, 80
whales, ix, 3, 4, 20, 51, 60, 61
whippet, 102, 117, 140
wild hunting dogs, ix, xii, 17, 58, 61–68, 75, 84, 141, 144
  and australopithecines, 65–66
  family orientation of, 62–63, 64, 65, 67
  genera of, 62, 63, 66, 144
  hunting technique of, 65
wild oxen, 75, 76, 90
wild pig, 67
wildebeeste, 61
wolf, vii, 46, 62, 72, 74, 75–82, 83, 102, 108, 110, 115, 120, 141, 144
  ascendancy of red fox over, in agricultural ecosystems, 47
  coat-coloring of, 79, 92, 93, 96
  communal organization of, viii–ix, 17, 70, 73, 78, 80, 82, 83, 86, 87, 88, 98, 130
  descent of domestic dog from, 17, 83, 88, 91–92, 93, 94–97, 98, 105, 130, 134, 139
  domestication of, viii, 83, 84, 85, 86, 87, 89, 92
  extermination of, 70, 75, 78, 81–82, 83, 130
  folkloric aspects of, 78–81
  gallop of, 100
  interaction with herbivores, 36, 75, 76
  interbreeding with coyote and domestic dog, 70–71, 83–84, 96, 106
  physical contrast with domestic canid, 84–85, 86, 90, 98–100
  as predator, 53, 75–80, 85–86, 88, 90, 98, 106, 114, 130
  range of, 46, 70, 73, 75, 81
  ritual muzzle-bite of, 87, 139
  "type" of, 91
Wolf, The (Mech), 75
wolfhound, 100, 102
wolverine, 21, 30, 32
"wood dog," 35
woodcock, 114
working dogs, viii, xii, 90, 91, 96, 110, 115, 119, 120, 130–31

Xoloitzcuintli, 117, 118, 119

Yorkshire terrier, 119, 120

zebra, 65
zorro, 55, 57, 142